The Century Kids

THE 1940s

POSTAL SAVINGS PLAN
for the Purchase of
UNITED STATES
DEFENSE
SAVINGS BONDS

Secrets

by Dorothy and Tom Hoobler

U.S. MAIL

The Millbrook Press
Brookfield, Connecticut

Photographs courtesy of FPG International: pp. 3 (bottom left), 15,
18, 20, 34, 43 (top left, bottom), 44 (top), 91, 161, 169 (Teresita,
Tony, Michiko), 171 (Freddy); AP/Wide World Photos: p. 6; Private
Collections: pp. 7, 25 (top), 26, 72, 78, 169 (Leo); © Underwood
Photo Archives, S.F.: pp. 11, 25 (bottom), 35, 40, 41, 43 (top right),
44 (bottom), 50, 171 (Polly, Molly); © Bettmann/Corbis: pp. 8, 13,
116, 145; Culver Pictures, Inc.: pp. 14, 156; Library of Congress:
p. 21; The Granger Collection, New York: pp. 22, 23, 124; Los Alamos
National Laboratory: p. 27; Archive Photos: pp. 37 (both), 65, 68, 82
(Hulton Getty), 125 (Scott Swanson), 137 (Hulton Getty), 140, 141,
149 (Reuters/Ho); 170 (David); Stock Montage, Inc.: p. 39; UPI/
Corbis-Bettmann: pp. 52, 114, 127; Anne Canevari Green: p. 55;
L. L. Bean, Inc., Freeport, ME 1-800-809-7057: p. 81; © Liaison
Agency: pp. 98 (Hulton Getty), 164 (Gene Peach); FDR Library:
p. 131; UPI/Bettmann: p. 133; Animals, Animals: p. 159
(© Stephen Dalton); © David Muench/Corbis: p. 163

In Memory of John T. Hoobler, U.S. Navy, 1942–1945

Hoobler, Dorothy.
The 1940s: secrets/by Dorothy and Tom Hoobler.
p. cm.–(The century kids)
Summary: In 1944 Gabriella, Esther, and other young people
see the impact of World War II on their lives in the United States.
ISBN 0-7613-1604-3 (lib.bdg.)
1. World War, 1939–1945–United States–Juvenile fiction.
[1. World War, 1935–1945–United States–Fiction.]
I. Hoobler, Thomas.   II. Title.
PZ7.H76227 Aaa5 2001
[Fic]–dc21 00-040199

Published by The Millbrook Press, Inc.
2 Old New Milford Road
Brookfield, Connecticut 06804
www.millbrookpress.com

ONE

An Idea

APRIL 9, 1944

I'll be with youuuu
In apple blossom time . . .

GABRIELLA HUMMED ALONG WITH THE SONG AS she washed dishes in the kitchen of the restaurant. The Andrews Sisters had so many hit songs, but this one was Gabriella's favorite. It made her happy and sad at the same time. Whenever she heard it she thought of the day her brothers and Jimmy left for the war.

That had been April 9, 1942—exactly 730 days ago. Gabriella had made a mark each day on the wallpaper next to her bed . . . that's how she knew.

The Andrews Sisters

After a while, she'd had to hide the marks by hanging a picture, so Mom wouldn't yell at her about them.

She didn't expect there were going to be so many marks. Everybody said the war would be over in a year. Now it was two years since they'd left, and it was still going on. War everywhere. People had started to call it World War II.

Tony was with the Marines somewhere in the Pacific. He didn't write very often, and said he wasn't allowed to tell where he was anyway. It was a military secret.

Leo and Jimmy were in England. That was a better place to spend the war, Gabriella thought. She liked to read about King Arthur and his knights. Queen Guinevere—that's who she'd like to be, with all the knights vying for her favor. In a way, when all the boys went off to fight the war, it was something like olden times. Because they were the same as knights except they used machine guns and planes instead of lances and horses.

Gabriella

She knew which knight she would give her favor to, but it was a secret. The only person Gabriella ever told was her best friend Angela. Angela swore she wouldn't tell, but she was Jimmy's sister so you never knew. It might slip out and then Gabriella would be humiliated forever.

Well Jimmy was gone for the duration, as people said. The duration meant as long as the war lasted. If it lasted long enough, Gabriella might have grown up into a gorgeous woman when Jimmy came home. And he would say, "Who's that gorgeous woman?" And then they'd get married and—

"Gabriella! You've been washing that same dish for ten minutes! Get your head out of the clouds!"

That was Mom. She didn't understand that Gabriella had dreams. All Mom ever thought about were Tony and Leo. In the front window of the restaurant was a banner with two blue stars on it. They showed that there were two boys from this family in the armed forces.

That wasn't so much. Down the block, the Angelottis had a banner with six stars. A couple of weeks ago, Mrs. Angelotti took down one of the blue stars and replaced it with a gold one. All the neighbors went to pay their respects. The gold one meant one of the sons had been killed. It was

Carlo. Gabriella hadn't known him very well, just to see in the street. But it made her scared anyway. If somebody on their block could be killed, maybe Tony or Leo, or even Jimmy. . . .

She shook her head. They'd come back. They all promised they would. And they looked so strong and young in their new uniforms when they left. As if nothing in the world could ever hurt them.

Gabriella scrubbed the dish she was holding very hard. All of a sudden, she didn't want to think about Jimmy and her brothers.

One of the other kitchen workers turned the radio on. It was 7:00 and time for *Charley's Chat*. Even though Charley and his guests were out in the dining room, the only way they could hear the program in the kitchen was through the radio.

As always, it began with the sound of Charley's watch. The tinkly music always sounded a little different to Gabriella each time it played. Sometimes it made her feel like dancing, as if she had to celebrate something happy. But at other times . . . the music made her a little sad, the way she had felt when Grandpop had died. It made her think of things that happened long ago, even before she was born.

Tonight the sound was a little scary to her. The show was broadcast overseas, to the army camps in England and the Pacific islands.

Gabriella imagined what it must be like for Tony, Leo, and Jimmy to hear the music. All of them knew exactly what Rocco's Famous Italian Restaurant looked like. They had been there for some of Charley's programs. And now they were far, far away, someplace where they might even get killed. Did the song scare them too?

Charley never let the song come to an end. His voice always cut in before it did. "Hello out there, all my friends," he said as he did every Friday night at 8. "Tonight we're going to chat with somebody who's been out to see the war. We're going to hear a firsthand account from somebody you all know . . . my cousin Harry Aldrich."

The people in the dining room applauded. It sounded like there were a lot of them. People liked to go out to eat, even though there was a war on, and a lot of people always came to see Charley's show.

As a matter of fact, it was Charley and his cousin Freddy—who was Pop's old friend—who persuaded Pop to change the name of the restaurant. It was just Rocco's Restaurant when he and Mom started it. But Charley said it sounded better when he read it on the air as Rocco's Famous Italian Restaurant. The radio network even paid for a new sign out front. Gabriella remembered when they put it up. Everybody was pretty excited about it, except maybe Pop. He said if it was famous, everybody would know it without having to put it in the name. And if people didn't see by the name Rocco that it was Italian, he didn't want them to eat here.

But he had to admit that business was good. Gabriella finished washing the last dish before a waiter could bring her any more. Drying her hands, she took off her apron and headed for the dining room. She wanted to get a peek at Harry Aldrich and see if he looked as good in person as he did in the movies.

He did. All over the dining room, people were standing up at their tables, trying to see him better. Fortunately, the kitchen door was pretty close to the stage where Charley and his guests sat. Gabriella had a great view of Harry Aldrich. He stood and waved as the applause went on, turning his head to look around the room.

Then his eyes fell on Gabriella. He gave a big smile, just like in the movies, and she felt it was just for her. She knew he was too old—he was even older than Pop! Anyway, she had sworn to be true to Jimmy, at least while he was in the war. But she was sure she'd never forget being smiled at by Harry Aldrich.

Harry

When the commotion finally died down, Charley started to ask Harry about the war. "I visited the troops in England last week," Harry said. "Saw the air bases there that we're using to send bombers into Germany. I thought about the role I played in *Wings Against the Axis*, as a pilot in the army air corps. Brave boys doing that job . . . flying out night after night in their B-17s, never knowing if they'll get back."

That was just what Gabriella feared, too. Except that Jimmy and Leo weren't pilots, so she guessed they were safe for now.

"What about the rest of the boys?" Charley asked. "There are probably lots of folks listening in tonight who have a son, a brother, a husband over there in England. We all know why they're there. They're getting ready to cross the Channel and take Europe back from the Nazis."

Harry cleared his throat. "That's right, Charley, but of course whatever I know about that can't be mentioned here." He lowered his voice. "We don't want to give away anything that might help the enemy."

Gabriella shivered. People were always warning about that. She saw posters with warnings like, "Loose Lips Sink Ships" and "Somebody Talked!" with a big arrow pointing at a man who had blabbed about a military secret.

She was pretty sure she didn't know any secrets. Even in the letters that arrived from Tony and Leo, certain parts had been blacked out. A censor read all the mail from servicemen to make sure they didn't reveal anything that might help the enemy.

"Well, of course we're not going to do that," Charley was saying. "But what message would you bring home from our boys overseas? How are they feeling?"

"I'd say they're feeling pretty blue," Harry told him. "They're far from home and they're lonely. They're out there getting ready to fight for our country." His voice gradually rose as he looked around the room. "We ought to get behind them any way we can."

The people in the restaurant cheered again. Harry went on, "Don't waste anything that could be used as war material," he said. "Drive your cars as little as possible. Ladies, give up those silk stockings that can be used as parachute cloth. Save all your tin cans, tires, and other scrap metal and rubber. And of course, no hoarding—make that meat, butter, and sugar go a long way."

Gabriella nodded through all of this. Her family did all those things. Because Italy was one of Hitler's allies, Mom and Pop didn't want anybody to think their family wasn't one hundred percent behind the war effort. On the day war was declared, Pop had sadly put away the Italian flag that stood next to the American one in the main hallway.

But Gabriella wanted to do something more. If she were older, she'd join the WAAC, the

Attention, Women!

JOIN THE WAAC
WOMEN'S ARMY AUXILIARY CORPS ★ U.S. ARMY
APPLY AT ANY U. S. ARMY RECRUITING AND INDUCTION STATION

Women's Army Auxiliary Corps. Mom just laughed when Gabriella said that, but she would.

Something Harry Aldrich had said gave her an idea. When the commercial break came, she went over to the broadcast platform. Of course, she had met Charley before, and he waved as he saw her coming.

"Here's a fan that I'm quite sure would like your autograph," Charley said to Harry as Gabriella arrived.

"No," she said, and then realized that sounded rude. Blushing, she added, "I mean, yes, I really would, but the thing is, I had an idea about how we could help the boys, the soldiers."

Charley

Harry Aldrich broke into a big smile again. His teeth were so white she felt like somebody was shining a warm light on her. "Well," he said, "you'd better tell us all about it."

"Well, you said some of the soldiers are lonely," she began. "That means a lot to me because my brothers and my best friend's brother are all overseas. You didn't meet Leo Vivanti or Jimmy Capellini while you were in England, did you?"

"No," he replied, "and I'm sure I would have remembered them."

A man in shirtsleeves leaned over the table. "Ten seconds to air, Charley," he said.

"You'll have to wait till after the program, Gabriella," Charley said.

Disappointed, she started to turn away. But suddenly Harry Aldrich took her arm. "Just a second," he said. "Charley, there isn't any reason why this young lady can't tell us her idea on the air, is there?"

Charley looked flustered. "We can't . . . there aren't enough microphones."

"She can share mine," said Harry. He gestured to the man in shirtsleeves, who was counting backwards on his fingers. "Hey, bring her a chair."

Things were a little mixed up for a second, but when they went on the air, Charley said, "Harry Aldrich is still with us, but now we've been joined by one of his many fans. Here's Gabriella Vivanti, whose father, by a strange coincidence, owns the restaurant that's been our weekly home since 1936."

Harry broke in. "She's here to tell us about her idea for helping the troops. And by the way, Gabriella, this is going out over the Armed Forces Network, so say hello to your brothers."

She gave him a grateful look. She had been nervous, but talking to her brothers was an easy way to get started. "Hi, Leo and Tony," she said, "and Jimmy too. We're all missing you and hope you come home soon. I bet Harry was right when he said you were lonely, except I write all three of you every week so I hope you get my letters. Mom writes too, and so does Jimmy's sister. Jimmy's mother sent a sweater for him."

Charley broke in, "That's great, Gabriella," he said. "Now I'd like to ask Harry—"

"She isn't finished," Harry said. Charley started to run his hands through his hair, nearly forgetting that he was wearing earphones. Glaring at Gabriella, he made a few quick circles in the air with his finger. She knew that was the radio signal for "hurry up."

"Anyway," she continued, "I bet there are a lot of soldiers who want letters and packages and maybe nobody writes to them. So I just . . . they can hear me now, can't they?"

"All over the world," Harry assured her.

"Well, if you sent your APO addresses here, maybe I could find somebody to write to you. I mean, I know lots of people who would."

Charley stared at her. "How are you . . . I mean, you could get a lot of letters."

"I think it's a great idea," Harry said. "And I tell you what. Are you listening, girls? In case Gabriella gets too many letters, why don't you send her your addresses too, and she'll mail you a serviceman's letter to answer."

Gabriella hadn't thought of that. It was perfect, but of course maybe she wouldn't get that many letters.

Two days later, 10,286 letters arrived at Rocco's Famous Italian Restaurant. And those were just the beginning.

Town Without a Name

| MAY 15, 1944 |

AMERICA WAS HARD TO UNDERSTAND, THOUGHT Esther. Every time she thought she had it figured out, her family moved someplace else that was completely different.

She remembered the trip when she and David first came here. That had been eight years ago, when Esther was only four, but she remembered going up in the air in the big balloon. Then the two of them stayed at Cousin Nell's house in California. That was nice, because it was near the ocean and the weather was sunny almost every day. Esther got to eat whatever she wanted to, because Nell didn't have any ideas about what was good or bad for children to eat. They often had ice cream at all three meals.

After Tony showed up one day, Esther had gotten the idea that Nell was running a kind of rich orphanage, and that there would always be more children to play with.

That didn't last too long, though. Pretty soon Mama and Papa came from Germany with Mama's parents. Esther wished they had moved in with Nell too. Her house had been big enough. But instead, they went to Chicago, where Mama and Papa both got jobs teaching at the University of Chicago.

So David and Esther and Tony took the long train ride together from Los Angeles to Chicago. Tony had come from there and decided he wanted to go back home.

Esther couldn't understand why anybody would prefer Chicago to California. It smelled bad some days, and Lake Michigan wasn't as much fun to swim in as the ocean. Worst of all was the cold, windy weather. The house Papa and Mama rented was a lot smaller than Nell's house. And they didn't get to see Tony as much, because his family lived in another part of Chicago.

Once in a while, however, Esther and David went up there to eat at Rocco's, his father's restau-

Esther

Chicago, 1940

rant. Really the food was better there than at Nell's house. Esther thought that if she were as rich as Nell, she'd eat at Rocco's all the time.

It was in Chicago that Esther first went to school. That was pretty interesting in some ways. Only the teachers expected her to stay back with the rest of the class. Esther just didn't want to do that. She was bored by those stories with one-syllable words like Dick and Jane and Spot the

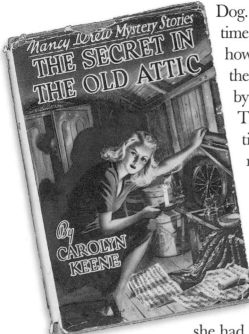

Dog. She couldn't remember a time when she didn't know how to read. She'd read all the Nancy Drew mysteries by the time she was six. They were no fun a second time, because now she remembered the plots.

And as for arithmetic . . . well, it was pretty obvious that 12 times 11 was 132, wasn't it? Esther thought geometry was much more interesting, but she had to teach it to herself.

Then the United States got into the war. It had broken out in Europe two years earlier. Esther's family were glad that England and France finally stood up to Hitler. But then Hitler conquered France and Denmark and a lot of other countries. Papa had a big map on the wall of his office. He kept track of the battles with pins and little pieces of string.

The only hope of defeating Hitler was for the United States to join the fight. But not everybody agreed that was a good idea. Some Americans felt that Hitler was no threat to America, so why get involved?

Esther remembered the evening when Papa and Mama had invited some other teachers from the University of Chicago for dinner. The party had turned into shouts and arguments about the war and whether the United States should get into it.

And then came a day that Esther would never forget: December 7, 1941. It was late Sunday afternoon when David came into the living room. He'd been upstairs listening to the radio. Esther saw that his face was pale. She remembered thinking maybe he was sick. "The Japanese have attacked Pearl Harbor," he said.

Hardly anybody knew where Pearl Harbor was, but Esther had been looking through an atlas

the week before. "Why don't the Japanese like Hawaii?" she had asked. But in the days that followed, everybody understood. The United States Navy had a lot of ships in the harbor, and Japan wanted to sink them. It did too, and killed thousands of American sailors as well.

The next day, almost everybody in the country crowded around a radio to hear President Roosevelt speak to Congress. Of course, Esther knew what he was going to say, but it made her feel stirred up inside to hear his voice. She had never seen the president, except for newsreels and newspaper pictures, but she knew he was very strong. You could tell.

He asked Congress to declare war on Japan, which it did right away. And then, because Japan was one of Germany's allies, Hitler declared war on the United States. So there were no longer any arguments about getting into the war.

That was when everybody's life changed. David decided he wanted to fight Hitler and signed up for the Navy. Esther and her friends at school started to spend their allowances on little green victory stamps with a picture of a Minuteman on them. They cost 25 cents, but you got this little booklet to paste them in. When you filled up the booklet, you could exchange it for a war bond. The money for these went to fight the war, and when the war was over, the government would buy them back, with interest.

25c	50c	75c	$1.00
$1.25	$1.50	$1.75	$2.00

$2.00 TOTAL STAMP VALUE $2.00

And then, almost two years after Pearl Harbor, Mama and Papa announced they were moving again. But it was a secret—the first of many secrets. Esther wasn't supposed to tell her friends at school, or even her teacher. She thought how strange it would seem when one day she just disappeared. She toyed with the idea of leaving a note in her desk suggesting that she had been kidnapped by Nazi spies. But at the last minute, she realized that Papa might be very annoyed if things got out of hand.

So early one morning she and her parents boarded a DC-3 airplane and flew west. After they got settled in, Esther asked, "*Now* can you tell me where we're going?"

"New Mexico," said Papa.

Jack

Sara

New Mexico? Esther knew it was the 48th and last state to enter the Union. But . . . "Why is that a secret? Why are we going?"

"Your father and I have new jobs there," Mama said.

"Teaching?"

"No." Mama smiled. "That's a secret too. We're not supposed to talk about it."

"War work?" Esther had *that* much figured out.

Her parents looked at each other over her head. She knew what that meant. If they were at home, they'd start talking in German, because they still thought she didn't understand it. But they couldn't talk German in public, not unless they wanted people to report them as Nazi spies or something.

They had to change planes twice and finally landed in Santa Fe. This was a different part of America. It looked very old and all the buildings were Mexican style—made of earth or yellow brick with stucco walls. At the hotel, they had Mexican food, spicy and full of cheese and tomatoes.

They didn't stay there long. The next day, a car picked them up and headed for the mountains in the distance. The driver wore a khaki army uniform with sergeant's stripes. For hours he drove through the desert on a road that never seemed to have any bends in it. The stark, flat scenery soon grew boring, after Esther got used to the cactus plants.

And then they spotted clouds of dust up ahead. Sandstorm, thought Esther excitedly. Like the ones she'd read about in tales of the French Foreign Legion.

Instead, it turned out to be just a military base, where jeeps and trucks with camouflage paint were raising the dust as they drove across the dry, sandy soil. The driver stopped at a checkpoint, where a metal bar blocked the road. A chain-link fence stretched on either side as far as Esther could see.

There seemed to be no reason for the fence. Nothing looked any different on the other side of it.

Their driver handed the checkpoint guard some documents. The guard peered inside the car, giving Esther such a stern glare that she tried her best to look innocent. Then he opened the gate and waved them through.

After another hour of driving, the road began to slant upward. Every so often, the driver had to turn sharply around a curve. On her side of the car, Esther looked down into space. She realized they were climbing the outer side of a steep mesa.

Magically, the countryside changed as they rose higher. They started to pass some juniper and aspen trees. Esther had seen some in a botany textbook. Mama pointed out from her side of the car, and Esther gaped at an abandoned ruin. Empty windows dotted the crumbling adobe walls. Long ago, she realized, Indians had lived here. She felt a chill, not of fear, but of awe at seeing the remnants of something very old.

As the car climbed the steep road, Esther could hear the engine whine. The driver kept downshifting, and a little steam rose up from the radiator. Finally, they crested a hill. Laid out before them was a town. Esther had never been so disappointed to see a place. It too had a fence and a gate to get through, but she couldn't imagine why anyone would ever want to go here.

Later on she learned that its name was Los Alamos. That was a secret, of course. Whenever they wrote to anyone outside, they had to use the address, "Post Office Box 1663, Santa Fe, New Mexico."

Before the war, the only thing at Los Alamos had been a boys' boarding school. When Esther heard that she thought they must have been very bad boys to be sent to such a desolate place.

The army had built a town here that wouldn't last as long as the old Indian village had. Esther and her family were lucky. They got an apartment in one of the wooden quadruplexes, where three other families lived. Single men and couples were assigned to one of the rows of trailer homes that stood on concrete blocks in a field. Most of the other buildings were large Quonset huts that were nothing but curved metal shaped like an upside-down U.

A small grocery store and a PX (where you could buy anything else) were the only places to shop. Once a week, on Saturday nights, a movie was shown in one of the mess halls where the soldiers ate. Sometimes there was a dance as well, but Esther never went. The boys she knew from school were more interested in playing war games than dancing.

The most important part of Los Alamos, of course, were the laboratories out in Pajanto

Canyon, a few miles from the town. No children were allowed in there, and very few women either. Esther's mother was one of the few women scientists, a fact Esther was proud of till a girl at school commented that it wasn't feminine to be a tech.

School in Los Alamos was very different from school in Chicago. Esther found to her surprise that there were children as smart as she was. In fact, all of the seventh graders knew more mathematics and science than their teacher, Miss Plumm. Miss Plumm was aware of this and didn't mind. She divided the class into teams and let them choose their own projects. For part of the day she read a chapter or two aloud from a book she had chosen. One of her favorite authors was Charles Dickens. Miss Plumm said that you shouldn't let science become your whole life, no matter how good you were at it.

The strangest thing about this part of America was not just that it was far away from everything else. Or that all the people who lived there were very smart. It was that nobody spoke about the reason they had all come here.

Everybody knew that the scientists at the labs were working on something very important, but you were never supposed to talk about it. You just acted as if it were perfectly normal to move out here to this made-up little town in the middle of the desert that was filled with army officers and people from Europe who spoke German and Italian and Hungarian.

Even the streets had no names. When the mail came, it was brought in a jeep by a soldier who knew right where the Aldrich family lived, even though the address was just P.O. Box 1663, Santa Fe, New Mexico—the same as everybody else's address.

Not that they got much mail. Grandma and Grandpa were living with friends in New York City, and didn't write often. Once in a while, a letter from David arrived, but he was in another secret base on an island in the Pacific Ocean. The letters from him looked like they'd floated ashore in a leaking bottle, and took months to arrive. Almost every sentence in them had something blacked out by the censor.

Besides David and her grandparents, the only person Esther ever wrote to was David's girlfriend Amy. Amy and David had wanted to get married, but they were too young when David joined the Navy. So they decided to postpone that till after the war.

Amy was working as a nurse in a military hospital in California. Esther liked her a lot, and knew Amy hardly ever got letters from David either. So the two of them had started to write back and forth, cheering each other up. At least Amy didn't ask why the Aldriches had moved to New Mexico. She must have suspected.

Anyway, even if Esther had told her, it would have been blacked out like the stuff in David's letters. Because it was almost certain that even the letters that civilians wrote at Los Alamos were opened and read before they went anywhere.

One day, Esther was walking home from school with Hans, whose family lived upstairs. "What do you think is the big secret that nobody is allowed to talk about?" she asked him.

"You're not supposed to talk about that," he pointed out.

For some reason, that made Esther mad. "I bet you don't even know what the secret is," she said.

His face got a little red, and he looked away from her. So of course she knew that he must know. It was right then that Esther decided she was going to find out the secret herself.

THREE

Air-Raid Drill!

MAY 20, 1944

BEN HAD BEEN IN A DEEP SLEEP, BUT SUDDENLY he was wide awake. Somewhere over his head a siren was howling. He jumped out of bed and reached for the light switch. Clicking it up and down, he found that it didn't work.

Then he remembered: In case of an air raid, you were supposed to keep all the lights off so the German bombers wouldn't be able to spot the targets on the ground. Uncle Georgie, the head air-raid warden, must have already thrown the main electric switch in the house.

More noises: doors slamming up and down the hallway. People shouting. "Georgie...." "Why won't the lights work?" "Who set off the siren?" "If this is another idiotic drill, . . ." "Where are my slippers?" "*Georgie*. . . ."

Ben almost didn't hear the sound of tapping that came from the door that connected his room with Iris's. He went over and opened it. In the moonlight from the window, he saw Iris standing there in her nightgown.

Ben

"I'm afraid," she said, taking Ben's hand. "Will we be killed by the bombs?"

"I do not think so," he told her. "I think this is only another drill."

"Must we go to the cellar again?"

"You are supposed to call it the bomb shelter. But I think yes, we must. We will be scolded if they notice we are missing."

Iris sighed. "I don't like it here in Maine," she said. "I wish we were back home in California."

Ben silently agreed, even though he knew that was impossible. He thought that although the Aldriches were very kind people, they were a little crazy. Of course he was too polite ever to say that. And besides, his family was deeply in debt to the Aldriches. Had it not been for them, Ben and his parents and sister would now be in a detention camp in Utah.

It had been a lucky day when his father found work as a gardener for Nell Aldrich. It was easier than farming, Father said, except of course that Nell was crazy. Ben saw now that this was because she was an Aldrich. Earlier he thought it was because she was a movie star.

Everybody understood that movie stars were not like anybody else. When Father went to work for her, Nell had stopped making movies. Ben couldn't understand why anyone would do that. It proved she was crazy, for it seemed to him that acting was the easiest thing you could do. And to become rich and famous for doing it.

Iris

But then Nell changed her mind. She had started to make movies again. Father said it was because some children came to remind her who she was. Ben was young when that happened, but he remembered when David and Esther and Tony arrived. The house in Santa Monica had been gloomy before then, but all it once it became lively. It was like the changes spring brought to the garden.

However, Nell's first new picture was nothing like what people expected. It wasn't like the old ones. Ben had seen some of her silent movies. She had a screening room in her mansion, and liked to have company when she watched them. So she let

Ben and Iris watch too. Ben was very young then, and the old movies had frightened him. Nell always got into trouble of some kind. In the end, she won out. But when the movie was over, Ben wondered how she could have escaped from such dangers. Sometimes he dreamed about them.

In her first new picture, however, Nell played a woman who falls in love with a man and then loses him. He went to war and was killed. It was very sad. Like everybody else, Ben kept waiting for the happy ending . . . the soldier had not been killed after all, or something like that. But no. It was very sad.

Even so, the new movie was popular, and Nell made another. In this one too, she lost her boyfriend. She played a woman who heroically gives up her love because she knew he could find more success without her. Ben thought it was icky, but Nell became more popular than ever. The newspapers said that she was acting out her own life. Because even though she was a beautiful, famous movie star, she had never married. Somewhere in her past, the papers said, she must have given up somebody she loved.

Ben was glad of one thing: When Nell became a big star again, she had lots of parties. He got to see all the big stars drive up in their fancy automobiles—Clark Gable, Bette Davis, Luise Rainer, Spencer Tracy, Nell's cousin Harry Aldrich, and many others. It was like living in a fairyland.

Clark Gable   *Bette Davis*

And then came the day that changed everything. Ben felt upset whenever he thought of the date: December 7, 1941. He and Iris had been playing outside the little cottage where they lived on the grounds of Nell's estate. Mother called them from the doorway. Ben thought it was too early for lunch, but that wasn't why she brought them inside.

Mother made them sit down. She put her arms around them both, making Ben afraid something had happened to Daddy. "The Japanese have attacked the United States," Mother explained quietly, "and now people will hate us."

Ben couldn't understand that at all. "We're not Japanese, Mother," he said. "We're Americans."

It was true that Daddy's grandfather was born in Japan. But he had come to California in 1888. His son was born here, so he was an American. And his son's son—Daddy—was born here, so he was twice American. And of course Ben and Iris never thought of themselves as anything but Americans.

But Mother was right. The next day Ben walked down to the beach, and somebody he didn't even know called him an ugly little Jap. Surprised, he was still thinking about that when he went into the candy store on the boulevard. Ever since he was allowed to walk to the beach by himself, Ben had spent his pennies there on Red Hots and jawbreakers and Kit Kats.

And today the owner told him to get out.

"What?" asked Ben. He wondered if the man thought he was going to steal something. Surely he remembered Ben had been there a thousand times before, and never stole.

"People won't come in here if I let you in," the man said. "Go back where you came from."

Go back where you came from. That was something they heard over and over in the weeks that followed. But the place where they came from was Mendocino County, where Grandfather Kenji and Papa's two older brothers worked on a farm.

They couldn't go back there even if they wanted to. Because in February 1942, President

Roosevelt ordered all the Japanese living on the West Coast to be "relocated." Ben hadn't heard that word before, and every time he heard it now he felt sick. Posters went up everywhere, telling people of Japanese ancestry to report for relocation. The government set up detention camps for Japanese Americans in isolated places out in the desert. The purpose was to keep them from doing anything to help Japan win the war. As if these Americans, just because they looked like Japanese, were dangerous.

All over California, "For Sale" signs appeared on Japanese-owned houses and stores. Ben's grandfather had to sell his farm—at a sacrifice price—when the government sent him and the rest of his family to a place called Topaz, in Utah. The day Ben's father heard about that, he went to Nell. He told her she should find a new gardener because he was going to have to leave soon.

"Why is that?" Nell asked. Father said she really didn't know. The newspapers had printed notices that the Japanese were being relocated, but Nell only read the entertainment news. So Father explained it to her.

"That's ridiculous," she said. "I need you here. I'll phone someone. Who's in charge of this relocation?"

But Nell found out, to her surprise, that nobody could help. Not even as a favor for one of the most famous movie stars in Hollywood.

Ben remembered that even his favorite radio program had to change. *The Shadow* was the only show with a Japanese character. The Shadow, who was really the man-about-town Lamont Cranston, had a Japanese chauffeur and house-boy named Kato. Or at least he did until December 7, 1941. After that, Kato became a Filipino from the Philippine Islands.

Kenji

So Father and Mother began to pack. All over the West Coast, Japanese Americans started to sell their houses and anything too large to take with them. They would have to leave a lot of things behind. But maybe, Father said, Nell would save them until . . . who knew? Someday when the war was over.

She did better than that. One day Nell came to their cottage while they were eating breakfast. Ben's mother was horrified because Nell never came here. Mother was worried that Nell would think the cottage was messy, even though Ben knew it was far neater than Nell's own house.

"I've made a decision," said Nell as Mother ran to bring her a cup of tea. Father and Mother looked anxiously at each other. Did this mean Nell was going to ask them to leave right away?

Nell

"I spoke to the Secretary of the Interior," Nell went on. "He told me that all Japanese families living in the Pacific Coast states must be relocated to the government camps. There are no exceptions."

Ben's heart sank. Secretly, he had hoped that because Nell Aldrich was so rich and famous, she could save them.

"Then I realized what the solution was," Nell went on. "We will simply all move to Aldrich House. For the duration."

41

Ben knew what "for the duration" meant—until the war ended. But where was Aldrich House? *This* was Aldrich House, to him.

He soon learned that Nell had another house—in Maine. That house too was near the ocean—just a different ocean, the Atlantic. So Ben thought it would be pretty much the same as the one near the Pacific.

It wasn't, of course. For one thing, Nell's parents, aunt, and uncles lived there. Most of them had been in show business too, but they had retired. Sort of. Because there was a theater at Aldrich House in Maine, and the Aldriches still loved putting on shows.

The older Aldriches were glad Nell was moving back to Maine. When she arrived, people in the nearby town had a parade in her honor. Mr. Pomeroy, the mayor, read a speech calling Nell, "Lake Chohobee Village's best-known daughter." For some reason, the older Aldriches found this very funny.

"Well, at least we won't have any trouble getting the fire department's approval for the next play," said Nell's father.

"Remember when Jack's fireworks display almost burned the place down?" chimed in Nell's Aunt Maud.

"With Theodore Roosevelt sitting right in the front row," added her husband, Uncle Nick.

Aunt Maud

Uncle Nick

They all roared at the memory. Ben didn't have the slightest idea what they were talking about, but he laughed too. He could see that life with the Aldriches was going to be fun, even if they were crazy.

They welcomed Ben's family, the Tamuras, as if it were the most natural thing in the world for Nell to bring them along. "Call me Uncle William," Nell's father told Ben and Iris. "You're part of the family now." Everybody else agreed.

Of course, Father still worked for Nell, so they told him he could

Uncle William

plant a victory garden. "President Roosevelt has urged everyone to grow their own food," Aunt Anna, who was Nell's mother, said. "But nobody has grown anything but flowers in our garden since Rocco left."

Ben's mother took over the cooking, which pleased everybody. The Aldriches' regular cook had found a job at a defense plant in Massachusetts. Of course, even here the war affected everything. And while on the West Coast people were afraid of the Japanese, here in the East they were worried about German Nazis.

Aunt Anna

Uncle Georgie was in charge of watching out for Germans. Mayor Pomeroy had appointed Georgie the official air-raid warden for this part of the town. Of course Aldrich House was the only house in this part of Lake Chohobee Village, but Uncle Georgie took his job seriously.

He had tied hundreds of helium-filled balloons to the ground all around the house. As soon as the warning came that German bombers were on the way, Georgie would release the balloons. Supposedly

Uncle Georgie

this would get in the path of the bombers and confuse the pilots.

"At least the balloons are attractive," commented Aunt Maud when she explained the idea to Ben and Iris.

From time to time—like tonight—Uncle Georgie would set off his air-raid siren to make sure everybody knew what to do in case of a German attack. They'd all had plenty of practice getting down the stairs in the dark. In fact, Iris wasn't the only one who was tired of doing it.

Ben finally thought of a way to persuade Iris to come down to the cellar, or the bomb shelter. "If you don't," he whispered, "maybe they'll think we're disloyal."

That got her going. In a few minutes they'd joined everyone else in the cellar, which smelled like some of the jars of preserves had broken. Peaches, thought Ben. Aunt Maud lit candles and set them on some empty shelves. That was regarded as safe because the cellar had no windows through which German bombers could see the light.

Georgie was the last one inside. He checked his watch, which had a radium dial that glowed in the dark. "Fourteen minutes and 23 seconds," he said, sounding slightly disappointed. "That's not much of an improvement over last time."

"It's quite late, Georgie," said Uncle William "Everyone is tired of these drills."

Uncle Georgie paid no attention. "Let's take roll call to make sure everyone's here," he said.

"We can see everyone's here," Aunt Anna pointed out.

"But in case of an actual attack," Georgie replied, "we might not have the candles, so we'd need to take the roll to make sure everyone is safe."

That didn't seem right to Ben, because the candles were stored down here. Aunt Maud made them herself from beeswax she'd collected and scented with wildflowers.

But like everybody else, Ben waited for Uncle Georgie to read the list of names, checking each one off as they answered "present."

Before he could finish, however, a new sound interrupted him. It was the big brass knocker on the front door upstairs.

Everyone fell silent. "Who could that be?" asked Uncle Nick. "It's nearly three o'clock in the morning."

"Georgie," said Aunt Anna in a threatening voice, "you didn't set off the fire alert, did you?"

"No," Uncle Georgie replied. "Maybe . . ." he added ominously, ". . . the Germans have landed at last."

FOUR

An Old Friend

IT WAS PRETTY CLEAR THAT GABRIELLA NEEDED help with all the letters that were coming in. At first she got the other girls in her class to volunteer to help. They would match a serviceman's letter with one that some girl had sent in. They tried to match up people who looked like they'd be good for each other. It started to be fun, because somebody would find a really good letter and read it aloud. Then somebody else read one that was a good match.

So they just couldn't keep up when there were more than ten thousand letters coming in every day. Besides, Gabriella soon realized that sending the letters back to people—with a three-cent stamp on each one—was going to cost a lot of money.

When Charley saw how popular Gabriella's idea had become, however, he got behind it in a big way. His sponsor—Bar-co-lean All-Purpose Cleaner—agreed to pay the cost of postage. Charley also broadcast an appeal for more volunteers to process the letters.

As a result several dozen teenage girls showed up at the restaurant the next morning. In Gabriella's opinion, most of them wanted to find a soldier or sailor's letter to answer themselves.

Every week now, Charley would have Gabriella on his show. "We really don't need any more letters," Gabriella told him when the microphone was off. "We're so far behind answering the ones we have."

"Just read some of the more interesting ones on the air," Charley told her. "Everybody loves what you're doing."

So she read a few letters she'd picked out of the pile. These were from servicemen, each thanking her for putting him together with a girl he liked. One was from somebody stationed in England. Gabriella liked to imagine he was in the same place with Leo and Jimmy.

"Dear Gabriella Vivanti," she read over the air, "You probably don't know how much enjoyment you brought to people, so I'm writing this to let you know. You gave my address to a real nice girl named Sue Ann Stephens, who lives in Texas. I guess because I'm from there too you thought we'd know each other. That's a joke.

"Anyway, she not only wrote me a real nice letter, she sent a Texas orange-pecan cake. It was Texas-sized too. I split it up and was able to give a piece to 20 of my buddies here in camp. Even though it was a couple weeks old, it tasted just like we were having it for Sunday dinner.

"So I wrote back and told Sue Ann how much we enjoyed the cake. I sent her my buddies' addresses and the next thing you know, Sue Ann had rounded up 20 of her friends to write to them.

"Well, I want to tell you that when the war is over, all of us are heading for McAllen, Texas. That's where Sue Ann lives. We're going to have the biggest celebration ever. And you're invited, Charley too if he wants to come.

"Sincerely yours, PFC Michael McNulty"

When Gabriella finished reading, Charley said, "That's a good idea. Sending food. Of course, you shouldn't send anything that might spoil."

A few days later, Gabriella came home from school to find an enormous pile of packages stacked at the bottom of the stairs to the Vivantis' apartment. They were addressed to her.

She opened one and moaned. It had a cake inside, and a note from some girl in California.

She wrote, "I'll bet my walnut carrot cake is just as good as any orange-pecan cake from Texas. Send this on to somebody overseas who wants a treat."

"Oh, nooooo!" cried Gabriella. "Don't send them to me!"

Just then Papa came out the door that led to the restaurant. He saw Gabriella's expression and laughed. "Why so upset?" he asked. "You've figured out something I never learned in twenty-three years in the restaurant business."

"What's that, Papa?"

"You don't have to cook your own food. Just say on the radio you'd like people to send you some." He snapped his fingers and grinned. "Just like that."

Rocco

"Papa, what am I going to do?" she asked. "We still can't keep up with all the letters coming in and there are over fifty volunteers. Now . . . these packages."

"You better call somebody smart," he said. "She'll tell you what you ought to do."

"Who's that?"

"Lorraine Dixon. She's a lawyer now, but she owes me a favor or two. Anyway, she's all right."

"You mean the colored girl who used to work here?"

"She had a lot of good ideas even then," he told her. "She made me get one of those cash registers that keeps a tape so you know how much money comes in. When she got into the University of Chicago, I offered to help her with the tuition money. But she got herself one of those things where the college lets you go free."

"A scholarship?"

"That's it. She musta been twice as smart as anybody else, because they usually don't give scholarships to Negroes or girls. Now I'd be happy if your brother Leo came back from the war and did half as well. He could get into Loyola. Father O'Rourke, the president of Loyola University, likes to eat here, and I never let him pay."

"What about Tony?" It bothered Gabriella that Papa always seemed to favor Leo over Tony.

Papa only shrugged. "He'll never amount to anything. He ran off that time and went to California. But he found out that life isn't so easy there either."

Gabriella had heard a very different story about Tony's trip—from Tony. But she didn't press the point. She had to do something about these packages.

"How do I get in touch with Lorraine Dixon?"

"She's got an office. I'll give you her phone number. Just tell her you're Rocco's daughter. She'll fix things up for you."

Over the phone, Lorraine sounded like she'd come from the South. But her accent was combined with a cheerful voice. Gabriella didn't feel shy about explaining her problem.

"I tell you what," said Lorraine. "Why don't you come on down to my office tomorrow? You can get here easy on the El."

Gabriella agreed. The next day was Saturday, and she set off bright and early for the address Lorraine had given her. It was on the South Side, in a Negro neighborhood. Gabriella felt a little self-conscious when she got off the El. Hers was the only white face in the crowd leaving the station.

In fact, a middle-aged woman stopped her and asked, "Child, you sure you got the right stop?" Gabriella showed her the address she'd written

The Chicago El

down. The woman's face brightened when she saw Lorraine's name. "You're here to see Lorraine Dixon? That's the right woman. She helps anybody who's in need. And let me tell you, child, she *really* helps. She don't take no guff from nobody."

The woman offered to take Gabriella to Lorraine's office. It wasn't far from the El stop. It was a storefront between a grocery and a funeral parlor. On the glass window were the words,

LORRAINE DIXON
LEGAL ASSISTANCE

But you could hardly read them because taped to the inside of the glass were a lot of posters and notices. It was like a community bulletin board.

"Go right on in," the woman told Gabriella. "You'll be glad you did."

Gabriella opened the door and saw a room with three desks that were piled high with papers and manila folders. At two of them, colored women sat typing rapidly. At the end of each line, they reached up to throw the typewriter carriage back, making a loud *thunk*. The *rat-tat-tat-tat* of the keys in between *thunks* sounded like machine guns.

Behind the third desk sat a young woman studying a book. Gabriella recognized her. It had been only a few weeks ago when Lorraine still worked part-time at Rocco's. Even then, on the nights when she sat at the cashier's desk, she used to spend her spare time reading.

What really caught Gabriella's eye were the drawings mounted on the wall behind Lorraine. There must have been at least a hundred. Some were in ink, others in watercolors, but quite a few were printed, full-color covers from comic books. Gabriella recognized one of them: a really popular comic book called *The Masked Crusader*.

Lorraine was concentrating so deeply on her book that she didn't notice Gabriella until she stood right in front of the desk. Then she smiled and said, "Why, is this really Gabriella Vivanti? You've gotten so much bigger!"

Gabriella must have shown her irritation. She was the tallest student in her class and looked like a string bean. Lorraine gave a little chuckle and said, "Tired of hearing folks say that, huh?"

Gabriella gave a nod. "I guess I'll get used to it," she said.

"Well, have a seat," said Lorraine, motioning to a metal folding chair by the desk. Gabriella looked down. A stack of papers was teetering on top of the seat.

"Whoops," said Lorraine. "Just put those on the floor. If you can find room on the floor. I'll know it's time to move when we can't find the floor any longer."

Gabriella moved the papers and sat, but her eyes wandered to the wall again. Lorraine turned in her swivel chair. "Like my art gallery?" she asked.

Some of the drawings were of people–just little sketches that seemed to catch someone's spirit with a few lines. At least two were of Lorraine herself. But Gabriella wondered more about the comic books.

"Why do you have the comic-book covers up there?" she asked.

"Don't you know? I guess you never met my brother Marcus. He draws *The Masked Crusader* books."

"He does?" Gabriella did remember Marcus, a little. Mom had framed a drawing he'd made of Tony, Leo, and Gabriella years ago. "I never knew that."

"Actually," said Lorraine, "the comic-book publisher doesn't want it known that *The Masked Crusader* is drawn by a Negro." She chuckled. "I just made sure when I drew up his contract that Marcus gets paid more than any of the white artists."

Lorraine moved aside some of the papers on her desk and pulled out a blank pad. "Anyway, let's see if we can help you out. From the way you described it on the phone, it sounds like you need to get organized."

Gabriella looked around, and thought that Lorraine was maybe the last person to give advice on being organized. But Gabriella admitted, "There's just too much to do, and I haven't got enough money for the postage to send all these packages and gifts overseas."

Lorraine made a note and asked, "This all got started when you went on *Charley's Chat*, right?"

Gabriella nodded. "I thought it was a good idea then."

"Oh, it is. It's a wonderful idea," said Lorraine. "Look how it's taken off."

She leaned back in her chair. "How is Charley? I haven't seen him in a long time."

"Oh, he's . . ." Gabriella hesitated, but decided she could tell Lorraine, ". . . sort of conceited."

Lorraine laughed. "You got that figured out. Here's what you need to do. Charley's sponsor . . . who is it?"

"Bar-co-lean All-Purpose Cleaner."

"Right. You have to get Bar-co-lean to hire people to sort these packages and send them out. There's too much work for volunteers. And rent some office space, keep track of what comes in and where it went. You can hire a secretary to take care of that. If anybody sends money, open a bank account."

Gabriella's head was swimming. "I couldn't do that. I'm . . . I'm just a kid."

Lorraine smiled. "We won't let anybody know that. You're smart enough to do it. We'll just let people think Charley is in charge of everything."

Suddenly Gabriella saw the point. She giggled. "He couldn't run anything like that."

Lorraine nodded. "But if you make believe he's in charge, he'll help us get the money."

FIVE

Message in Code

HANS AND TWO OTHER BOYS WERE PRETENDING TO be B-29s. With their arms outstretched like wings, they were running in circles and making noises like RRRRRR-KSSSHH! and RATATATATA TATA! Around and around they ran in the front yard of the quadruplex, destroying German cities that were actually anthills.

Esther was getting a little annoyed because she was sitting on the front porch trying to read *Lost Horizon*. The story reminded her of Los Alamos. In *Lost Horizon*, an explorer stumbles on the valley of Shangri-la somewhere in Tibet. It had been cut off from the outside world for centuries. Gradually,

the explorer realizes that in Shangri-la, nobody ever grows old.

The secret of Los Alamos was different from that, she was sure. But even so, every day was pretty much the same as the one before, as if nothing would ever change.

It seemed that things only changed in the outside world. Today everybody was excited about the news. June 6 had been D-Day, the day when the Allied Army crossed the English Channel and landed in France. This was the start of the invasion that everyone hoped would free Europe from Hitler.

That was why the boys had turned into B-29s. In fact, the invasion was the topic of conversation everywhere in Los Alamos. Many of the scientists and their families had fled Europe to get away from Hitler. Everybody was hoping that the invasion would succeed. Esther had heard some of the girls at school talking about the time when they might go home. For them that meant back to Europe, but Esther didn't feel like Europe was home anymore.

Despite the news, all the adults went about their work—their secret work—just as they did every other day. Esther wondered for the thousandth time what was going on in the laboratories in Pajanto Canyon. Whatever was going on, it wasn't necessary for the invasion of Europe.

Esther hadn't made much progress since deciding to figure out what the secret was. She had taken a peek at a book Papa had been reading. It was in German, but she understood enough to know it was about atoms and molecules. Papa had always been interested in those, so that was no surprise to Esther. He had often told her that atoms were the basis for everything. He called them "the bricks God used to build the universe."

Of course there were many kinds of atoms, some large and some small. This book was mostly about uranium and plutonium. They were elements. Esther had to look them up in an English-language chemistry book but didn't learn much more.

Now, on the front porch, trying to read her book, she heard one of the boys say something strange. "An atom bomb!" he shouted. "I'm going to drop an atom bomb right on Hitler." All at once the two other boys shushed him, and the three of them began to wrestle. They fell on the ground in a tangle of arms and legs, laughing and shushing each other.

An atom bomb, thought Esther. Could that be the secret? Every now and then, out in the desert, there was an explosion. But people were told it was just a dynamite blast, and it wasn't very big. Esther didn't know how big a bomb explosion really was, but the ones in the Movietone news-reels at the theater looked bigger than those blasts in the desert.

She took out the secret notebook she kept with her at all times. She even put it under her pillow at night. Because it contained everything she knew or guessed about the secret of Los Alamos. Now she turned a fresh page and wrote:

ATOM BOMB??

In a little while, the boys continued their game. They buzzed off down the street, going back to base for refueling. That meant they were headed for the PX, where you could buy ice-cream cones. Except they weren't made with but-terfat like the ice-cream cones that you could get before the war. They tasted like frozen skim milk with a tiny bit of flavoring.

Then a jeep came slowly down the street. In it was the soldier who delivered the mail. He wasn't at all like the nice mailman they'd had back in Chicago. Whenever Esther was sitting on the front porch, the soldier would always say, "I have some mail for your parents. Is anyone home?" As if Esther weren't someone to be trusted with the task of giving her parents the mail.

Today, however, he brought something else. The jeep stopped, and the soldier walked to the porch carrying a thin envelope. By the kind of paper and the markings on it, Esther could see that it must have come from David. He was the only serviceman they ever got mail from.

The soldier stopped in front of the porch and asked, "Are you Miss Esther Aldrich?"

"Yes, I am," she replied. As if he didn't know from delivering the mail all the time they'd been living here.

He handed her the envelope as if it hurt him to do so. As she looked at it, she wondered why David was writing to her. His letters were usually addressed to the whole family.

She waited until the soldier had gotten back in his jeep before opening it. The first thing she noticed was that the letter had been typed. David usually handwrote his letters. He said that he liked to lie in his bunk and think of home as he wrote them.

Strangest of all, the letter didn't seem to make any sense. Oh, it *did* if you thought that David had completely changed. He went on and on about a poem he was thinking of writing. He asked if she remembered the Pacific Ocean near Nell's house. He reminded her how they thought Lake Michigan in Chicago was so different from the ocean.

Esther began to worry. She'd heard of battle fatigue, in which soldiers went crazy from the strain. But as far as she knew, David had never been in a battle. Earlier, he'd said the Navy was going to teach him Japanese. David had always been good with languages.

But then, in the very last line of the letter, David left a clue. "Sometimes I think about the game we played with messages the first summer we lived in Chicago. That was fun. Do you remember?"

Of course she did. David had worked out a code that he and Esther used to send secret messages. They would leave them in hiding places in the new apartment their parents had rented.

And now . . . David was telling her that this letter was in code too! Esther set to work figuring it out. It wasn't hard. That was the reason David had typed the letter—so it would be easier to decode it.

She held the paper up to the sun. Light shone through the tiny pinholes David had made above some of the letters. Writing these down and separating them into words, Esther soon had the real message:

> If you can read this, you're still as smart as ever. I wanted you to know that I've finished figuring out Japanese code messages. I volunteered to join a group that is going to parachute into

China. I got tired of sitting around an office while others are risking their lives. Of course I couldn't tell you this in a regular letter because the censor would cut it out. If you don't hear from me for a while, tell Mama and Papa what I'm doing. You have a job too—help them finish their work so we can win the war sooner. David

Esther felt tingly when she read the letter. Before now, she knew David had been in a pretty safe place. She could understand why he wanted to get into some real fighting. But parachuting into China? She knew that the Japanese army occupied large parts of China, but the rest of it was dangerous too.

Esther took the big world atlas off the shelf. She wished David had given some more details.

Parachuting into China

China was a big country. She put a thin piece of paper over the map and started to trace it. From now on, she was going to follow the Pacific war in the newspapers.

Then she remembered. What about Mama and Papa? What should she tell them? Thinking it over, she decided that David wanted her to keep his message a secret for now. There was no sense worrying Mama and Papa unless it was necessary. That was why David told her and not them.

However, her parents noticed Esther's sudden interest in the Pacific war news. On her map, Esther included all of Southeast Asia and parts of the Pacific Ocean. That was where the real fighting was going on. Marines and army units were attacking small islands that were held by Japanese troops.

On her map, Esther marked the latest American victories that summer—the islands of Saipan and Guam—with stickpins flying little American flags.

"I'm just curious," Papa said one evening, "why you aren't following the Allied army across Europe?" It was a good question. The children at school all talked about the European battles, not the Pacific ones.

Esther replied, "Because the Pacific is where David is, isn't he?"

Papa nodded. "Yes, but he's probably at a headquarters post."

A question had been nagging at Esther, and she blurted it out. "Are there any American soldiers in China?"

Papa's brow furrowed. "I don't think so." He paused. "Well, perhaps there are some secret units that are working behind the lines."

More secrets, thought Esther. "What does 'behind the lines' mean?" she asked.

"It means they're not where the fighting is. They are trying to organize civilian resistance groups or spying on Japanese installations."

"That would be very dangerous, wouldn't it?"

"Oh, yes," said Papa. "For one thing, it would be almost impossible to get out of there until the war ended. And if the war ended badly. . . ." He trailed off.

"You mean if we lost the war?" she asked. Nobody ever talked about that. It was too scary to think about.

"We won't lose the war," Papa said firmly. He seemed about to say something else, but then changed the subject. "We're having a guest for dinner tomorrow night," he said.

"Who?"

"Dr. J. Robert Oppenheimer, the man who invited us to join the project here."

Dr. J. Robert Oppenheimer

"Oh," Esther said. "I'm surprised he has a name."

"Esther," said Papa in his "warning" voice, "All this secrecy . . . there's a reason for it."

Sure, she thought. But even Hans and his friends knew the scientists are building atom bombs. She wondered what Dr. Oppenheimer would say if she casually asked him when the atom bomb would be ready.

She didn't, of course. Esther had learned that she could find out more by listening quietly to adults who thought she didn't understand what they were talking about.

For instance, "it." That was what the three adults kept discussing at dinner. Esther had a feeling that even if she weren't there, they would still talk about "it" rather than say its name out loud.

Dr. Oppenheimer turned out to be a thin, lanky man who looked as if he only ate when somebody reminded him to. His intense eyes darted only once or twice in Esther's direction, but she had a feeling that her face was now in a filing cabinet in his mind. If they met again in twenty years, she was sure he'd remember her.

Dr. Oppenheimer and Papa were having a disagreement over "it." Papa seemed to have doubts about it. That wasn't like him at all. Esther had never seen Papa when he wasn't absolutely certain that he was right.

It was hard for her to tell just what he doubted now. At first she thought he worried that whatever they were making wouldn't be finished fast enough. "The Germans must be working on it too," he said. Dr. Oppenheimer agreed.

But Papa seemed to be afraid of something else about it. "Maybe it won't stop," Papa said to Dr. Oppenheimer. "The reaction could spread beyond the target and destroy everything."

"We've considered that in the calculations," Dr. Oppenheimer replied. "It will be very powerful, but not limitless."

Dr. Oppenheimer sat back in his chair and lit his pipe. "In any case," he said, "if you are a scientist you cannot stop such a thing. If you are a scientist you believe that it is good to find out how the world works."

"I have always thought so," Papa responded. He glanced at Esther. "But now . . . when I think of my children, and their future, I wonder if there are some things it is better not to know."

Esther didn't understand that at all.

Watching for Nazis

MAY 20–JUNE 15, 1944

IN THE CELLAR OF ALDRICH HOUSE, THERE WAS A lively discussion as to whether or not someone should go upstairs and answer the door. If it really were a troop of German soldiers, then it didn't seem like a very good idea.

"But," Aunt Maud pointed out, "the Germans wouldn't bother to knock, would they? They would just . . . pillage, or whatever it is they do."

"Break a window, at least," suggested Uncle William.

"I think I'll have a look-see," Uncle Nick said finally. "Can't hurt, one way or the other."

"If they capture you," warned Uncle Georgie, "they'll torture you to find out where the rest of us are."

"I'll just have to risk it," Uncle Nick replied. He even took a candle with him.

In a few moments, they heard another voice along with Uncle Nick's. A woman's voice.

Uncle Nick called down the cellar steps, "All clear! Who do you think it is? Peggy, of all people. And what do you think she's brought us? English marmalade and scones! Come upstairs and let's all have some."

Peggy

Peggy turned out to be Nell's older sister. She had once been a screenwriter, but since the war began had become a foreign correspondent. After Georgie turned the electricity on and a fresh pot of coffee was brewing, Peggy took a look around. Her eyes fell on Ben's family.

"You must be the Tamuras," she said.

They all nodded and smiled.

"Nell wrote me a letter when she was trying to keep you out of the camps. I called a few friends of mine in Washington but they weren't able to help. I never thought of bringing you here."

Ben tensed up. He hoped she wasn't going to say it was too dangerous for the Aldriches to let the Tamuras stay.

"Have you had any trouble with the Pomeroys?" Peggy asked.

"Actually," said Uncle William, "Marshall Pomeroy became mayor after his father retired, and he organized a welcome-home parade for Nell."

Peggy laughed. "He must have something to hide." She turned to Ben and Iris. "All the same, if anybody in the town asks you kids, just tell them you're Chinese."

Ben thought she was joking. He snickered.

"I'm serious," said Peggy, pointing at him.

"But . . ." He hesitated. "No one would believe that. Anybody can see the difference between a Japanese and a Chinese person."

"Not in Maine they can't," said Peggy. "All you have to remember is that Chinese are our allies and Japanese our enemies."

Ben didn't like hearing that. Once more he wanted to say, "I was born in California, and I'm an American."

"Tell us what you've been doing, Peggy," said Uncle William. "We read some of your articles in the Boston *Globe*. We thought you were still in England with the troops."

"Well, as you know, by now they've invaded France," she said. "I applied for a press pass to go along, but they aren't giving any to women. I told them it was up to me if I wanted to risk getting killed, but the answer was still: No women allowed. They're afraid we'll do a better job than the men. The Germans bombed us while we were in England. What's the difference if we go to France and they bomb us there?"

"You're too old to be running around in the middle of all that terrible fighting," her mother said.

Peggy snorted. "I wasn't going to fight, Mother," she said. "I just wanted to see what's going on and write about it. Anyway, I decided I wasn't going to sit around in England. I came back to look for a story in the States. I heard an interesting rumor."

"There's not much of a story in Lake Chohobee," said Uncle Nick. "Unless you count the German spies that Georgie is always on the lookout for."

"They're not imaginary," Georgie retorted. "The body of a German was found on the beach up at Cundys Harbor."

"They thought that was just a sailor from a submarine," said Uncle Nick.

"Well? You don't think the Germans might invade in submarines?"

Aunt Maud broke in. "You could do a nice article on our victory garden, Peggy," she said. "Kenji and the children have done a wonderful job. Ours will be the largest victory garden in the area."

"I'm not looking for that kind of story," said Peggy. "I came back here because I want to find Jack and ask him some questions."

"Jack?" They all looked at each other. "Are you sure you don't mean Harry?" asked Aunt Maud. "He has a new movie out."

"About German spies," added Uncle Georgie with satisfaction.

"No, it's Jack I want to see," said Peggy. "He's involved in a project that could win the war, from what I hear."

"Well, he brought his family here from Germany," recalled Uncle William. "They stayed out in California with Nell."

"No, that was just the children who stayed with Nell," said Aunt Maud. "She was in her child-collecting phase then. She even had one of the sons of that little Italian boy with her."

"You're living in the past, Maud," said Uncle Nick. "Rocco is forty-four now, the same as Nell. And both his sons are in the army."

"Oh, that's terrible," said Aunt Maud. "Sending such young children to war."

"They might use them to spy on the Germans," suggested Georgie.

"I'm looking for Jack," Peggy reminded them in a firm voice.

"I remember now," said her father. "They lived in Chicago. What were his children's names?"

"Esther and David," said his wife.

"Yes. And Jack taught at the university there. His wife did too. She had a college degree."

"Oh, she had more than one degree," added Uncle Nick.

Aunt Maud sighed. "In my day we didn't need degrees. We just took care of the house and children."

"Maud," said Uncle William, "you were on the stage from the time you were six. This is the only house you ever lived in, and we've always had servants."

"I don't think you should speak that way in front of the children," said Aunt Maud.

Uncle William and Uncle Nick looked at each other. They raised their eyebrows and made circles around their ears with their fingers.

Ben was confused, but he knew an opportunity when he saw it. Taking Iris's hand, he said, "We must excuse ourselves now." He wanted nothing more than to get back to bed. He bowed in Peggy's direction and said, "We are very pleased to meet you, Miss Aldrich. We're glad you weren't a German soldier."

As they turned to go, Peggy said, "Don't bow to people, or they'll think you're Japanese."

In the morning, almost everybody slept late because of the excitement the night before. Ben's mother got up with the sun as she always did. She fixed oatmeal with maple syrup for Ben and Iris.

Ben just poked at his bowl. "Eat up," said Mother. "You're lucky to have it. There are starving children all over the world."

He knew that. She mentioned every time he didn't clean his plate. "Mother," he asked. "Do you think we'll have to leave here now?"

"Why would you ask that?" she replied. "The Aldriches have been wonderful to us."

"But that Peggy . . . she acted like we were . . . you know."

"Nell invited us here. You should feel grateful."

"But she's gone. She went out to California to make a movie. Maybe—" He stopped abruptly, because Uncle Georgie had appeared. He never seemed to need much sleep. Ben's father said it was because his brain didn't turn off.

"Oh, I'll make your omelet right away," said Mother. That was what Uncle Georgie had for breakfast every morning, along with a glass of prune juice.

Uncle Georgie sat down at the table. Ben wondered if he'd heard what they were talking about.

But he acted as if nothing was wrong. He unfolded the linen napkin at his plate, shook it out, and then folded it back in a different pattern. Ben and Iris watched him, because they always thought he was going to do some kind of trick with the napkin.

Mother returned with the omelet. Uncle Georgie liked it cooked so that it was still runny inside. He looked up at Ben and Iris. "I'm going down to the beach today," he said. "Want to come along?"

They looked at Mother and she nodded. "No swimming," she said. "Still too cold in the water."

"Oh, we wouldn't think of swimming," replied Uncle Georgie. "We're going to watch for German submarines." Ben's heart skipped a beat.

Mother frowned a little. "Yes, maybe," she said, "but don't try to catch one."

Gasoline was one of the many things that were rationed during the war. Each family received ration books with stamps inside. Every time they bought gasoline, they had to exchange some stamps for it.

However, Uncle Georgie had fixed up the family's 1937 Packard so that it could run partly on alcohol. There was a large metal tank attached to the rear of the Packard. Inside was what Uncle Georgie called a converter that turned alcohol into fuel. That way, he didn't have to buy very much gasoline.

The only trouble was, the Packard didn't run very well on alcohol. It took Uncle Georgie a long time to start it. He kept lifting the hood to adjust settings, then running back to the metal tank to turn valves.

Ben didn't mind, because Georgie let him watch and explained what he was doing. When Ben climbed back inside the car, Iris asked what was wrong. "The doohickey needed tightening because the thingamajig wasn't letting enough air into the whatchamacallit," he said proudly.

Finally the motor did start, although maybe the fact that the sun had warmed up the engine had something to do with it. Uncle Georgie released the hand brake, engaged the clutch pedal, and the Packard lurched down the driveway.

Iris turned and looked out the back window. "Is smoke supposed to be coming out of the converter?" she asked.

"That's only water vapor," said Uncle Georgie. "Just cleaning out the tubes." He swerved then to avoid another car that was bearing down on them. The other driver honked his horn and roared down the main road.

"That's the Pomeroys' LaSalle," Uncle Georgie said. "They were traveling pretty fast—a lot more than 35 miles [56 kilometers] an hour, I'd say." To save gasoline, all drivers were asked not to go any faster than that. "But they never seem to have trouble getting enough gasoline."

They saw few other cars on the way to the ocean, although Uncle Georgie had to downshift when they followed some slow-moving trucks. One of them was a tanker filled with liquid of some kind. Uncle Georgie crept along behind it for over a mile before the truck turned left into a long driveway. They could read the sign on the side: MILK.

"Hm," said Uncle Georgie. "That's a little odd."

"Why?" asked Ben.

"The Pomeroys live up there," Uncle Georgie replied, "and they don't use enough milk to have it delivered by tanker truck."

"There's a Pomeroy Super Market in the town," piped up Iris. "Mother goes shopping there. They must use a lot of milk."

"That's true," said Uncle Georgie, "but they wouldn't have it delivered to their house."

At any rate, the road was clear now, and they were able to travel a little faster. In half an hour, Uncle Georgie turned the Packard onto Beach Road. A fresh breeze was blowing in from the sea, which looked choppy. The sky was gray too. Only a few families and children had spread their blankets and towels on the sand. There was a white wooden beach house where people could change into their bathing suits, but nobody was using it.

Before getting out of the car, Ben and Iris took off their shoes and socks. Uncle Georgie kept on his L.L. Bean rubber-soled boots, pointing out that keeping your feet dry was a good way to avoid toenail fungus.

Ben and Iris decided they'd risk it. It felt good to have the sand between their toes again, even if it was wet and cold. There was a lot of seaweed on the beach, brown and shiny, and Ben and Iris avoided stepping on it. But Uncle Georgie started to poke around in it with a stick of driftwood he'd picked up.

A wave hit the beach, and Iris laughed as the surf ran up the sand and over her feet. Just as Mother had warned the water was still very cold, even though it was June. In California by now, Ben realized, the temperature would be over 80.

Uncle Georgie reached down and picked something out of a clump of seaweed. It glittered in the sunlight.

"What's that?" Ben asked.

Uncle Georgie showed him the piece of twisted silver metal. "It looks like a belt buckle," he said. "Maybe one from a German sailor." He took out a pair of binoculars and began to search the horizon. Ben looked out there too, but all he could

fishing trawler

see was a fishing boat casting its nets and some bobbing wooden floats.

"Look for a periscope," Uncle Georgie told him. "Anything sticking out of the water."

Ben pointed out the red-and-white floats.

"No, those are buoys to mark lobster traps," said Uncle Georgie. "My eyes aren't as good as they used to be. I wish I had a sonar detector so I could see under the water."

Ben smiled. "That would help fishermen too."

"Fishermen!" Uncle Georgie snapped his fingers. "Ben, you've just given me one of my best ideas."

Ben was pleased. He didn't know how many Aldriches would have shaken their heads in dismay if they heard Uncle Georgie say that.

A Staring Contest

OCTOBER 1944

LORRAINE ARRANGED EVERYTHING JUST AS SHE had promised. Every week now, Gabriella gave a report on *Charley's Chat.* She told how many letters and packages had come in, and even read some of the better letters. At the end, following Lorraine's advice, Gabriella thanked Charley and the Bar-co-lean All-Purpose Cleaner Company for making all this possible.

"The folks at Bar-co-lean know that the war will be won at home as much as it is on the battle-field," Charley always responded. "And that reminds me . . . listeners, in your home, don't you want to win the war against dirt and germs? Well, then Bar-co-lean is the army you want to send into battle."

With the money from Bar-co-lean, Gabriella was able to rent an office. Lorraine found her a woman who took care of all the details like sorting the mail and bringing all the packages to the post office. In addition to her volunteers from school, Gabriella now had half a dozen secretaries to read the letters and match them up. She even hired some high-school boys to pack all the things that people sent for the servicemen overseas.

Pop came to the office now and then to look things over. "I told you Lorraine would give you good advice," he said. "You've got quite a setup here."

"It's hard keeping up with it all," Lorraine said, "but it's exciting."

"I know," he said, nodding. "It's like when your mom and I started the restaurant."

Pop looked at her in a certain way, like when he was tasting a new wine, trying to decide whether to buy some. "You know," he said finally, "you could maybe think about going to business school—unless you had other ideas."

"Pop," she said, "what do you mean, other ideas?"

He shrugged. "I don't know. We'll see what happens. There's a war on, you know. But don't work so hard. You shouldn't let your schoolwork slip, you know?"

She nodded. That had been a problem at first. But then her teacher, Miss Wilkes, volunteered to help open letters one Saturday. And she found some that she decided to answer herself. Miss Wilkes had such a good time that she told Gabriella that working on this project would count toward her grades–which turned out to be the best in the class.

But Pop seemed to be talking about more than just schoolwork. Gabriella wished he would just come out and say what he meant. With Tony and Leo, he always did–maybe too much. Anyway, he put the idea of business school in Gabriella's mind. She liked it. Next year, when she started high school, she could get started taking business courses.

Wednesday came, the night when Charley's show was on. The newspaper headlines had made everybody more excited about the war than usual. In Europe the Allied invasion had been a success. After landing in France, the troops had marched all the way to Paris, taking it back from the Nazis. People were saying the war would be over by Christmas.

Most exciting of all, in the pile of letters that arrived that day, one had been for Gabriella. One of the secretaries realized it was from Gabriella's brother Leo and brought it to her. Gabriella couldn't have been more thrilled, unless the letter had been from Jimmy. She tore it open and began to read:

Dear Sis,

Well I just wanted you to know we all have been hearing you on the radio. We're still in camp. I can't tell you exactly where, but you can probably figure it out from the fact that everybody in town talks with an English accent. Ha ha. By the time you get this, though, we might be somewhere else. Nobody knows where. That's the army for you. They have a word for it—"snafu." It means, "Situation Normal, All Fouled Up."

Anyway, I'm pretty famous because people found out I'm the brother of the kid who's sending out letters and packages from girls in the States. They all want me to ask you to match them with a good-looking girl. Don't worry about that. Believe me, they are all good-looking to us guys over here.

You remember Jimmy Capellini? You and his sister are such pals. Anyway, he sent a letter in after he heard you on the radio, and guess what? You found him somebody he likes. A lot! She lives in New York and when he wrote back, she sent her picture along with some great biscotti. They were almost as good as the ones Mom makes. Anyway, she wants him to visit her family when he comes back from the war. I think something may develop—if you know what I mean. Ha ha.

Anyway, give my love to Mom and Pop and tell them I'm all right. I just thought you might get a kick out of reading a letter about one of your success stories.

Love,
Leo

Gabriella felt tears come to her eyes. She'd never even seen the letter from Jimmy Capellini, or she'd have written a reply herself. Biscotti! She knew how to make biscotti. Mom made the best biscotti in Chicago, and showed Gabriella how.

She shook her head. The girl who had given her the letter came over and asked, "Are you all right? There wasn't any bad news in the letter, was there?"

She meant did anybody die or get wounded. No, Gabriella wanted to say, I just arranged for somebody I love to find a girlfriend.

But of course she didn't say that.

"Everything's all right," she said bravely. She thought about Ingrid Bergman giving up Humphrey Bogart in the movie *Casablanca*, which Gabriella had seen three times. Ingrid Bergman did it to help win the war—at least, that was the way it seemed. She had to go with this other man. It was confusing, but very romantic.

So Gabriella rubbed her teary eyes, and said, "Let me have some more letters. All these guys are waiting for a reply." She sat down and thought that Jimmy would never know the sacrifice she had made for him.

Gabriella was still thinking about it that evening as she got ready for the broadcast of *Charley's Chat*. She wondered if there were some way to let the

A Scene from Casablanca

audience know she'd made a tragic personal sacrifice, without going into detail about it.

But another surprise awaited her. A strange woman was sitting across from Charley at the broadcast table. Gabriella usually recognized Charley's guests, but couldn't place this woman. She wore what looked like a man's striped shirt, only with a scarf instead of a tie. She was smoking a cigarette and looked as if she were giving Charley a scolding.

Gabriella couldn't help smiling. Everybody wanted to give Charley a scolding, but he was so full of himself that nobody tried.

As Gabriella came closer, the woman looked up at her with sharp dark eyes. Gabriella almost turned and left, afraid she would get a scolding too.

"This is Gabriella," Charley said to the woman. "She's the one who takes care of the letters and packages for me."

The woman held out her hand. Gabriella shook it, feeling a little awkward. "I'm Peggy Aldrich," said the woman. "Call me Peggy when we're on the air."

"Yes, Miss Aldrich," Gabriella replied. She was trying to remember which one of the Aldriches Peggy was.

"I'm Nell's older sister," Peggy explained, seeing Gabriella's confusion. "And Harry's cousin. You do know them, I suppose."

Gabriella nodded.

"Everybody knows movie stars," Peggy said with a laugh. "I'm only a journalist."

"Oh!" Gabriella said. "Now I know who you are. You write a column in the *Tribune.*"

Peggy looked a little pleased. "That and 387 other newspapers."

"But . . . I thought you were overseas with the troops."

"I got as far as England," Peggy told her. "But they wouldn't let me storm the beaches of Normandy. Too old and too female."

Gabriella wanted to ask if Peggy had visited the camp where Leo and Jimmy were, but Charley interrupted. "We're going on the air in 30 seconds," he said. "Have you got a report ready, Gab?"

"Yes," she said, annoyed that he had to ask. She always had her report ready.

"We'll use that in the second segment of the show," Charley told her. He motioned toward Peggy. "She wants to go first."

So why did I have to rush to get here on time? Gabriella thought. Anyway, Peggy looked like she'd have something interesting to say.

Charley popped open the case of his pocket watch, and it started to play the strange little tune that began the show. The show's producer knelt in front of the broadcast table and counted off the last ten seconds on his fingers.

They were on the air. Charley let the tune play a little more and then announced, "Welcome once again to *Charley's Chat*. This is Charley Norman Jr. broadcasting live from Rocco's Famous Italian Restaurant in Chicago." He reached over to close the case of the watch, and continued. "Tonight my first guest is the noted journalist and writer Peggy Aldrich."

93

Peggy's hand suddenly shot out and took the watch from Charley. He gave her a surprised look, but they were on the air so he couldn't say anything.

Charley stumbled and then resumed, "Um, Peggy Aldrich, who writes the newspaper column, 'A Woman's I.' She has recently returned from England, where she visited some of our servicemen who right now are fighting in France. Peggy, have you got any messages from the boys?"

"Charley," Peggy replied, "do you remember when I gave you this watch?"

Charley waved frantically at her, pointing at the microphone and mouthing the word, "ON."

"You were six years old and you found the box the army sent back when your father was killed."

Gabriella stared at Peggy, wondering what this was all about.

"You were always a little snoop," Peggy went on. "Of course you got that from me. I like to find out things too."

Gabriella blinked. Peggy was . . . Charley's mother? Charley didn't seem like he ever had a mother.

"I think we're a little off the topic," Charley said. He looked at Gabriella as if she had just appeared. "Here's Gabriella Vivanti with her weekly report on all the letters that have come in from the boys overseas." He jabbed his finger at her and pointed to the microphone.

"Oh, we can hear that later," said Peggy, pulling the microphone closer. "I want to tell you something, Charley."

"Later, Mother," he said through clenched teeth.

"Did you hear that?" Peggy asked, looking at Gabriella. "He never calls me his mother."

"You never wanted me to," Charley blurted out.

"I didn't want to be reminded of your father," she said. "He was a good man, a brave man, and he volunteered to fight for his country. I gave him the watch because I thought it would keep him safe. But it didn't."

"Mother, if you want the watch back. . . ."

"No, that isn't what I want," she said. "I want you to be as brave as he was. What are you doing here, Charley?"

His face turned bright red. Gabriella was afraid his head would burst open.

"I failed the physical when I went to the draft board," he said in a loud voice. "My eyes aren't good enough."

"Charley," she said, "that's no excuse."

They stared at each other for a few seconds. Nothing was going out over the air, and the producer kept waving his hands. He caught

Gabriella's eye and motioned for her—anybody!—to start talking. Because you can't have a staring contest on the radio.

Gabriella started to clear her throat and then remembered that you aren't supposed to do that in front of the microphone. "Last week," she began, "one of the most interesting letters came from. . . ."

EIGHT

Bad News

DECEMBER 1944

ESTHER SHOULDN'T HAVE KEPT A NOTEBOOK. SHE realized that too late. But it made her feel as if she were making progress. Every time she found out something about the secret of Los Alamos, she wrote it down. One day, she even followed the mail carrier's jeep on her bicycle. She wanted to see if he went inside the barbed-wire fence to the dark green buildings where the laboratories were. He didn't.

She pasted newspaper articles in the notebook that she thought might be about "it." In August the Germans had started bombing England with something called "robot bombs." These were big bombs that flew on aircraft that didn't need pilots.

"Rockets," Papa said to Mama. "The Nazis have rockets powerful enough to carry bombs. If they had 'it,' they could destroy a whole city with one rocket." Esther wrote the words DESTROY A WHOLE CITY in her notebook next to ATOM BOMB. She wondered: Could that really be true? Maybe she didn't hear right.

That news made everybody at Los Alamos nervous. For a while Esther thought maybe the scientists were working on rockets. But nothing ever flew overhead, so she decided that couldn't be it.

She thought a lot about what an atom bomb must be. At first she guessed it must be a large and

Robot bomb over London

important bomb, since there were so many scientists working on it. On the other hand, she knew atoms were very small. So maybe an atom bomb would be so tiny that it could be dropped on the enemy in a small plane. Like the radio-controlled model airplane that David had built when they lived in Chicago.

One day, Hans came up behind her when she was sitting on the porch writing in her notebook. "What's that?" he asked.

She immediately closed it. Of course that was the wrong thing to do. It only made him more curious.

"Just some notes," she said. "For school."

"I thought it was your diary," he said. "You're always writing in it."

"Nothing happens around here," she replied. "There wouldn't be anything interesting to write in a diary."

"Well, what are you taking notes on?" he asked.

"None of your business," she said, biting her tongue almost as soon as she said it. Because now Hans would devote his life to finding out what was in it. So she couldn't take the notebook to school anymore, and had to write in it mostly at night in her bedroom.

That was the only time when her parents were home, and Mama liked to come in often for a heart-to-heart talk. Esther didn't know why. She guessed Mama felt a little guilty about the fact Esther was home alone so much.

"Are you having a good time in school?" Mama asked one evening.

Esther gave her a look. Did anybody have a good time in school? "It's better here than in Chicago, Mama," she said. "The children are smarter than the ones in Chicago."

"That's one advantage of living here," Mama said. "But I know it's been difficult for you."

Esther shrugged.

"Someday," Mama said, "after the war is over, we'll settle down in a nice place. You'll make friends."

"When will that be?" asked Esther.

Mama seemed surprised. "Why . . . soon, I hope. You know the Allies have taken back France and have crossed the Rhine into Germany. It shouldn't be much longer."

"But David is in the Pacific. What about that part of the war? The newspapers say the Japanese will never surrender."

"Once the war in Europe is over, Japan won't be able to hold out alone. It will be a relief to your papa, because they won't have to use. . . ." Mama trailed off.

"Won't have to use it?" Esther asked. "Is that what you mean?"

Mama just smiled, looking a little sad as she did.

"Mama, will you tell me something?"

"Why certainly, Esther." Mama seemed happy that Esther was going to ask a heart-to-heart question.

"Is 'it' an atom bomb?"

Now Mama wasn't so happy. "That's one name for it," she said softly. She sat on Esther's bed for a long moment, thinking. "Esther," Mama said finally, "do you remember the story of Pandora?"

"Pandora?" It seemed familiar. Then Esther remembered. Pandora was from Greek mythology. "She opened a box and let all sorts of horrible things out."

"Yes," said Mama. "All the troubles and cares of the world. But that wasn't the point of the story. Why did Pandora want to open the box?"

"Well . . . wasn't it because she was curious?"

"Yes," Mama said. "And even though she was warned never, never to open the box, her curiosity was too strong."

"Oh," said Esther. She saw the point. She felt a tiny bit ashamed.

"Someone told me that you're keeping a notebook," said Mama.

Abruptly, Esther's mood changed. "Who told you that?"

"Someone who meant well. You see, Esther, even the scientists are required to leave all the notes on the project in their offices and laboratories, where they'll be safe."

That's why I couldn't find any around here, Esther thought. "It was Hans Dichter, wasn't it?" she asked. "The little tattletale."

"Hans's mother told me," said Mama. "And it was only because she was concerned. If General Groves found out you had this notebook, your papa and I might have to leave Los Alamos."

"Mama . . . it's only things I've written down for fun. How could I know anything that was important?"

"You have big ears and a good head, *Liebchen*," said Mama, using the affectionate German word. "I noticed that when Dr. Oppenheimer was here, you made an excuse to go upstairs. Was that to write down something he said?"

Esther felt her face grow warm. Mama must watch her a little closer than she thought.

"Yes," said Esther, "but what he said was *right*." She quoted it by heart: "'If you are a scientist, you believe that it is good to find out how the world works.' That's all I'm trying to do, Mama. Los Alamos is my world and I want to find out what's going on in it."

Mama sighed. "I know that is natural for you, Esther. But you must give me the notebook."

Esther felt strange, almost dizzy. Mama couldn't ask her to give up the notebook. She had written down everything. David's letter was pasted onto one of the pages, opposite the decoded version that she had written out.

Esther shook her head. "Mama, I can't. . . ." She struggled to think of an excuse. "It's really sort of a diary. I have my personal thoughts in it." Mama wouldn't make her give up her diary, would she?

Apparently not, because Mama pressed her lips together and thought. "You must burn it then," she said finally. "We will do it together. I won't read any of it."

Esther hung her head, then nodded. "All right, Mama. As long as you won't read it. Do you want to do it now?"

"It's better to get it over with," said Mama.

So Esther went to her room to get the notebook. It was on her desk, next to a stack of her schoolbooks. As she reached for the notebook, she knew she couldn't go through with it—no matter what. On top of her schoolbooks was a small green notebook, the kind that was held together at the spine with black paper tape. Holding her breath, she picked up the green notebook instead. . . .

They went to the backyard, where Mama crumpled up some old newspapers and put them in the metal can that was used for burning trash.

Esther placed the notebook on the newspapers. Mother struck a match. In a few minutes, the flames licked over the top of the can. Mother stirred the papers with a stick so that everything would burn.

The fire attracted attention. Esther looked at the upstairs window of the quadruplex. Hans and his mother were watching.

Afterward, Mama took Esther to the PX for an ice-cream cone. Esther felt a little guilty as she ate it. But she had something else to think about: Who was she going to find to lend her the notes to recopy for history class? Not Hans, anyway. She didn't want him wondering what had happened to her history notebook.

Snow arrived early in Los Alamos that year. It made the ugly buildings look pretty for once. The children threw snowballs in the playground, and Esther made sure to take aim at Hans.

Classes let out early for the Christmas holidays. At home, Esther concentrated on following the Pacific war, wondering what David might be doing in China. She sat and looked at the map, trying to guess what part of it he might be in.

The Aldrich family hadn't received any more letters from him, and Esther's parents began to worry. She listened to them trying to reassure each other.

"I guess David's too busy to write," Mama would say cheerfully, after Papa turned off the radio news at 8 P.M.

"It's a long way across the Pacific," Papa might reply. "His letter could have been on a ship that sank."

"The censors hold everything up," Mama reminded him. "They're being very careful not to give away anything."

"Probably we'll come home one day and find three or four letters from him, all written weeks apart," Papa said.

When she heard them talking like this, Esther wondered if she should tell them what David had written to her. He had told her not to let them worry. But on the other hand, she couldn't show them the letter, because she had pasted it in the notebook that was supposed to have been burned. And anyway, knowing that David was somewhere in China would just make Mama and Papa worry more.

On New Year's Eve, her parents had a party. Esther knew they were still worried about David, but it was important to keep up morale.

Morale meant you were supposed to keep on doing dumb things just as if there weren't any war or you weren't worried about anybody you knew getting killed. At school, for example, a WAAC sergeant came to teach the girls physical education. She apparently thought they were all going to join the army, because she led them in calisthenics and running over an obstacle course. All the boys gathered to watch and had a hilarious time making fun of the girls in their gym suits getting red in the face and all out of breath.

It was just about as goony as that, Esther thought, to have a New Year's Eve party when there was a war on. But that afternoon she helped Mama make canapés. They cut cheese into little cubes and stuck colored toothpicks in them; they wrapped slices of bologna around cream cheese; and they put little sardines from a can across the tops of sliced hard-boiled eggs. Esther thought if it were her party, she'd make hot dogs and hamburgers.

Mother got out a fresh linen tablecloth and spread it over a card table in the living room. Esther began to carry out the canapés and arrange them nicely on plates. She heard the noise of a car engine stop in the street outside. Thinking one of the guests was arriving, she went to tell Mama.

"Probably the Skidmores," Mama said. "They're from England and always arrive early. Open the door and take their coats."

The doorbell rang and Esther went to answer it. But it wasn't the Skidmores. It was the soldier who delivered mail. Only now he held a yellow envelope with the distinctive WESTERN UNION marking on it.

A telegram.

Esther felt cold all over when she saw it because she knew what it meant. She had heard of other families who received telegrams during the war.

She even forgot to be annoyed with the soldier when he said, "I have a telegram for your parents. Is anyone home?"

Papa stepped out of the bedroom, still tying his tie. He stopped when he saw the soldier holding the telegram. Because he knew too.

Papa held out his hand. "I'll take it," he said. The soldier handed it to him, glad to get rid of it.

Papa waited until he'd left before opening the telegram. Esther could hear the thin paper tearing. In the kitchen, Mama had the radio playing. It was an opera, and the singer sounded very sad.

Mama came out then, smiling and carrying a tray of Vienna sausages, which were almost as good as hot dogs, but not quite. Esther saw and heard all these things so vividly that they were like a photograph. Time seemed to have stopped.

Mama's smile disappeared when she saw Papa's face. And then the telegram in his hands.

"David is missing," he said.

Esther went numb. She knew that whenever someone was missing, it meant they were dead.

Searching for Submarines

MARCH 1945

UNCLE GEORGIE WAS DRIVING PRETTY FAST, BEN thought. Particularly since it was midnight and he didn't have the headlights on. Ben pointed this out, thinking maybe Uncle Georgie had only forgotten. But no. "There may be a blackout without our hearing about it," said Uncle Georgie. "We wouldn't want to make ourselves a target for the German bombers.

"Anyway," Georgie went on. "it's perfectly safe. I know these roads like the back of my hand. And there won't be anyone else driving on them at this time of night."

That was true. They hadn't met another car since leaving Aldrich House. At first Ben had thought it was quite an adventure. And it showed he was a patriot too, because what could be more patriotic than hunting for German spies in the middle of the night.

It did make him a little uneasy not to be able to tell his parents what he would be doing. "Not even Iris," Georgie had warned him. "Or anyone else in the house. Loose lips sink ships." That was from a poster they'd seen in front of Pomeroy's Super Market. It meant that somebody's careless talk might be overheard by an enemy. That could give them information they could use to sink a ship crossing the Atlantic.

Just how, Ben wasn't sure. But everybody seemed to believe it, so it must be true.

Uncle Georgie wouldn't even have told Ben about the spy mission if it wasn't for the fact that he needed somebody to help load all the equipment into the back of the old Packard.

There was another reason why they hadn't met any other cars on the road. Because gasoline was rationed, no one could buy enough to go driving just for the fun of it. Uncle Georgie, of course, could drive whenever he wanted in the Packard that he had converted to run on alcohol.

The car slowed as Uncle Georgie spotted bright lights up ahead. "That's the Pomeroys again," he said with annoyance. "It's a disgrace. Him the mayor of the town—wasting electricity like that. I think I'll just give him a piece of my mind."

Uncle Georgie pulled the car to the side of the road and shut off the engine. "You can wait here if you want," he told Ben. For a second Ben listened to the sounds of insects all around them in the darkness. He decided he'd rather follow Georgie than be left alone.

Instead of walking back along the road, they headed into the pine woods alongside it. The terrain sloped sharply uphill, and Ben kept slipping on old pine needles. Georgie reached the top of the hill before him.

When Ben caught up, Georgie shushed him. "What do you make of that?" Uncle Georgie asked.

Down below them was the Pomeroys' house. Floodlights on poles lit up the backyard, where a big tanker truck was parked. Like the one they'd seen last year. The truck was painted with the letters MILK. Right now, a man in coveralls was connecting a black hose from the truck to a pipe sticking out of the ground.

"It looks like the truck is delivering milk," said Ben.

"How is the milk delivered at Aldrich House?" asked Uncle Georgie.

"Well, the milkman brings a few bottles and maybe some butter. He leaves them in the insulated box by the kitchen door."

"Take a deep breath," said Uncle Georgie.

Ben did, and wrinkled his nose. "That's not milk," he said at once. "It's . . ."

"Gasoline," finished Uncle Georgie. "The Pomeroys are hoarding gasoline."

Hoarding meant buying up large quantities of anything that was rationed. Some people had rushed to the stores at the beginning of the war and bought up all the sugar, coffee, and tea that they could. It was one reason why the government made people use ration stamps for things that were in short supply.

"But how could anybody hoard gasoline?" asked Ben. "They couldn't get enough ration stamps for that much gasoline."

"They're storing it in a tank in the ground," said Uncle Georgie. "And as for getting it, money talks. Did you ever hear of the black market?"

"No," Ben replied. "Is it open at night?"

"It's open all the time," Uncle Georgie told him, "and it operates wherever people want to buy something that is needed for the war effort." He shook his head. "I'll have to think what to do about this."

"Shouldn't you report them?" Ben asked. "I mean, the gasoline is needed for planes and tanks and other army stuff."

"That's right. But it's going to hurt morale in the town when people hear the mayor himself is a hoarder. I think I should give him a chance to turn himself in."

Uncle Georgie looked at his watch. "We're just wasting time here. There's no need to confront Pomeroy now. The proof is in the ground, should we ever need it."

They made their way back to the car and headed for the ocean again. "I guess it's time to tell you my plan," said Uncle Georgie.

Ben was hoping they would get around to that. Uncle Georgie had told him earlier that a good soldier has faith in his commander. Besides, if Ben didn't know the plan, he could hardly give it away, could he? Even so, Ben wanted to know just what they were going to do.

He expected that Georgie wanted to set up some kind of observation station. When German spies came ashore they probably did it at night, when it would be easier to hide.

But Georgie's plan was grander than that. "If you look on a map," he told Ben, "you would see that the logical place for a submarine to come ashore is at Burton's Cove. The drop-off

German submarine

there is steep, so a sub could get quite close to the shoreline.

"What I have made," he went on, "is a net that we will stretch across the mouth of the cove. I've rigged up a crude motion detector with insulated wire that will tell us if any metal objects strike the net."

Ben thought this over. "How are we going to get out there to spread the net?"

"I moved the family boat up here last week. It's small, only a twenty-footer, but it will serve our purposes."

The boat was named the *Board of Avon*. Ben asked about that, and was sorry he had. "Shakespeare was known as the Bard of Avon," said Georgie. "Father wanted the boat to be named that. But the painter thought he'd made a mistake, so he painted *Board of Avon*. Father thought that was quite a joke, since when actors are on stage they are said to walk the boards. So he left it the way it was."

It took them a while to move the netting from the car into the boat. The net was bulky and Georgie had to fold it just right so they could let it out over the side at the mouth of the cove.

Finally Georgie brought aboard a wooden box with a crank and some electric terminals on the side. "We'll attach the wires on the end of the last piece of net to these," Georgie said. "There are batteries inside that will power the detector."

"And then, we're going to wait for . . . a submarine?" asked Ben.

"I assume that's how they'll arrive," Uncle Georgie said. "A surface ship would be too visible."

"But how can you be sure that it will arrive tonight?"

Uncle Georgie pointed to the sky. "New moon," he said. "Darkest night of the month. The war in Europe is going badly for Germany, so tonight is one of Hitler's last chances to strike back at us directly."

It sounded right when Uncle Georgie explained it, Ben thought. He shivered as he thought of Hitler

Hitler and staff review map of Europe.

standing over a table with a map on it. As his generals watched, he put his finger on the map, pointing out the attack spot: Burton's Cove.

"We're the first line of defense," said Uncle Georgie. Ben felt a surge of pride and hoped that someday he would be able to tell Mother and Father what he'd done.

Before Uncle Georgie started the boat, he put on a cork-filled life jacket and made Ben do the same. "If anything happens," Georgie said, "try to get to shore and spread the alarm."

Ben nodded. He hadn't thought about their boat being attacked. He was going to ask a question when the engine roared into life. It was right beneath them, in the stern of the boat, and the noise made talking almost impossible.

They chugged out toward the open sea. The moon was just a sliver high in the sky, but once Ben's eyes got used to the darkness, he could see the near side of the cove's mouth. A single tall pine tree grew atop a rocky point there. Ben had been here before. He knew that on the far side, which was shrouded in darkness, there was a wrecked boat that had been blown onto the rocks by a nor'easter years before.

When Georgie reached the pine tree, he cut back the engine and motioned to Ben. Together they lifted one end of the long net. It was heavy because there were lead weights in it. But they managed to push it over the side. As it sank to the bottom, more of the net unfolded and followed. Uncle Georgie showed Ben how to control it so that it didn't tangle.

"The rest should be easy," said Uncle Georgie. "We'll cross the mouth of the cove, letting out the net as we go. Can you hold it while I take the helm?"

"I think so," said Ben.

It was a little tricky at first. But he soon got the hang of it, letting the net unfold by itself instead of trying to hurry it along.

Ben glanced ahead every now and then, hoping to catch sight of the other side of the cove. But there was nothing ahead yet but blackness. The sea and the sky ran together like a dark curtain.

Then he caught a glimpse of something else. At first, it was hardly any lighter than the black sky and water. Then Ben worried that it might be a rock. But that was impossible unless they'd gone way off course.

He turned the other way and shouted, "There's something up ahead of us!"

Uncle Georgie saw it. He cut back on the throttle and fumbled with something in his jacket. It was a pair of binoculars. Holding the tiller with one hand, he brought them to his eyes.

Ben looked forward again. Their boat was still heading toward the shiny gray object floating in the water. It was large, he could see now—larger than the *Board of Avon*. And it seemed to be getting bigger.

He heard Uncle Georgie yelling at him, and looked back. Georgie was gesturing for him to come to the stern. Ben let the net drop and ran.

"It's a submarine," Georgie yelled above the sound of the engine. "Take a look!" He handed Ben the binoculars.

They weren't much help, because the lenses were spotted with water. Anyway, they just magnified the darkness, and Ben couldn't tell what he was looking at.

"Are you sure?" he asked Uncle Georgie.

"One way to find out," Georgie replied. He reached across the control panel and flipped a switch. Two searchlights mounted on the front of the boat suddenly cut through the darkness.

Ben saw the light reflect off the metallic surface of the object. Then, a long thin tube seemed to rise up from it.

"Periscope," said Georgie. "They've spotted us."

Ben didn't know what to think. All this had seemed like an adventure to him until now. But the thought that a submarine full of real Nazis was right in front of him . . . he couldn't comprehend it.

"I'm going to ram him," said Georgie. "Save yourself and sound the alarm. Swim toward the closer end of the point."

"What?" said Ben.

"No time," explained Georgie as he shoved Ben over the side. Underwater, Ben could hear the boat's engine roar up to full throttle. Spitting water and gasping, he came to the surface. He realized the life vest would keep him afloat no matter what happened.

He turned his head in the direction of the engine. Since the boat's lights were still on, he could follow its progress. But it was difficult to see the gray object it was headed for.

Suddenly the lights dimmed. Ben could hear glass shattering and the scraping of wood against steel. Then a jet of flame shot into the air and the boat seemed to disintegrate.

The noises echoed off the rocks all around the cove. If anybody is nearby, Ben thought, they're sure to hear that. They'll bring help.

Gradually the sound died away, however. The flame hissed and went out in the water. The engine was dead, and now the night seemed darker and quieter than ever.

"Uncle Georgie!" Ben shouted. "Can you hear me?"

There was no answer.

TEN

The Gabriella Show

SPRING 1945

GABRIELLA HAD A LOT OF SUPPORT FOR HER FIRST show. Mom and Pop said it was nice somebody in the family was now doing the broadcast, and told her to be sure to mention the address of the restaurant.

Freddy Aldrich—Pop's old friend who had given Charley the show in the first place—was there. He agreed to let Gabriella take over the show, but waiting for the first broadcast to begin, he looked nervous. He kept reminding Gabriella about things she already knew. Like watching the producer, who would tell her when to break for commercial. Pop pulled Freddy over to a table, and poured him a glass of wine.

Lorraine arrived too, and she knew just what to say to make Gabriella relax. "Don't think about being too young for this job," she said. "Freddy is vice president of the network, and he's not putting you on the air because he's a friend of your father's. He's doing it because people liked your talk about the letter-writing campaign."

"But what if everybody tunes in to hear Charley, and they find me?"

"Charley's been off the air for six months. The replacement show didn't do well. The network got a lot of mail from listeners wondering why they stopped having you on. And anyway, you can tell people that Charley has just gone to war and he'll be back. That is where he went, right?"

Gabriella smiled. "I think so. The last we heard, he was on his way to France. He said he'd cover the war as a correspondent, even if he couldn't get into the Army."

"Was his mother happy about that?"

"I'm not sure. She's a strange person. She couldn't get permission to go into combat areas, but she had another story in mind. When she was here, she wanted to find her cousin Jack Aldrich. I guess she must have found out where he is, because she disappeared."

"I see you have Charley's watch to start the show." Lorraine pointed to the old silver pocket watch, its case closed now, that rested on the table.

"He left it behind," said Gabriella. "Do you think it will be all right for me to play the music from it to start my show?"

"Why not? Wouldn't Charley want you to do that?"

"I don't know. He just forgot it, when he and Peggy were arguing. You know, I found it with the case open. That meant the song had finished. He always told me that would bring bad luck. Do you believe that?"

Lorraine smiled. "Charley and I used to talk a lot about luck. I think you get some bad luck and some good. But life depends more on how hard you work. I've seen you work, Gabriella, and I don't think you have to worry."

"Thanks," said Gabriella. "You want to be on the show? Harry Aldrich is going to be here, and he promised to bring Clark Gable."

"Nobody would want to hear *me* when you've got those two heartthrobs on," said Lorraine with a laugh. "Maybe I'll come on sometime when it's snowing hard and nobody else will show up. Then you can call me."

"Thanks," said Gabriella, "for even thinking the show will last till winter. Papa was right. You're a friend."

The producer leaned over and said, "Ten seconds to airtime, Gabriella." He started to count down on his fingers, and Gabriella opened the watch cover. The song began.

The show went a lot easier than Gabriella had feared. Harry Aldrich liked to talk, and when he wasn't talking about himself, he interviewed his friend Clark Gable. That was just as well, thought Gabriella, because she was in awe of the famous movie star. She'd seen *Gone With the Wind* eleven times.

LIMITED ENGAGEMENT...
FULL LENGTH. NOTHING CUT BUT THE PRICE

DAVID O. SELZNICK'S
production of
MARGARET MITCHELL'S
Story of the Old South

GONE WITH THE WIND

IN TECHNICOLOR. *starring*
CLARK GABLE

Gable had actually served in the armed forces. Many people thought he enlisted because his wife Carole Lombard had been killed in a plane crash. "Clark didn't just sit at a desk in Washington shuffling papers," Harry told the audience. "He flew bombing missions over Germany, with antiaircraft guns aimed right at him. Tell us what that was like, Clark."

"Wasn't anything special about it," Gable said. "I signed up because I wanted to fight for my country, like everybody else. If they put me in a plane, I was ready to fly it."

U.S. bombers over Germany

"Sounds like you think I should sign up and do some fighting," said Harry.

Gable chuckled. The sound melted Gabriella's heart. "No, Harry," he said. "You're too old. They'd have to put you in a wheelchair."

"Watch that, Gable," growled Harry. "You and I will be putting on the boxing gloves if you keep that up."

Gable smiled because he knew Harry was kidding. "There's a part for everybody to play in the war effort," Gable said. "You're making movies that bring up everybody's morale. And look at all the women who've taken jobs in factories to make planes and tanks while their husbands have gone to war."

Gable turned to Gabriella, who'd been listening like a mouse under the stove, glad nobody noticed her. Just having Gable look at her made Gabriella nervous. "And our hostess tonight is doing a terrific job too," he said. "When I was in England, I knew a dozen fellows who got letters because of this program." Gabriella tried to speak, but her mouth just opened and closed without a sound.

"You mean to say Gabriella didn't send you a letter, Clark?" Harry asked.

She could feel her face get so hot that it must look like a stop light. People in the restaurant laughed at first, but then they started to applaud. Clark Gable reached over and touched her hand.

Mail call

He gestured toward the customers. "That applause is for you," he said.

It was a miracle she was able to get through the rest of the show.

Everybody who worked opening letters and packages had heard the program, of course. The next day they all had questions when Gabriella walked into the office. "What was he like?" "Did you get his autograph?" "Do his ears look that big in person?" "Why didn't you ask him if he's ever going to get married again?"

Gabriella was a star at school too. And the next week, Freddy came up to her before the broadcast. "We got some nice mail about the program," he said. "People liked it. Keep up the good work."

But the best thing that happened was still to come. About two weeks later, the Vivantis got letters from both Leo and Tony. They'd heard the program too, on the Armed Forces Radio Network. Gabriella read Leo's letter first:

Here I am in France. I guess that's no secret now. Anyway, I heard my kid sister on the radio and learn she has her own show. And she's chumming around with Clark Gable, no less. The guys in my platoon are telling me Gabriella's going to be the mayor of Chicago by the time I get back. I'd say ha ha except maybe it's not a joke.

Well, I'm sitting in a foxhole with a poncho pulled over the top. Rain is coming down outside and there's mud sliding down my neck. All I want right now is to sit down at the big table by the door to the kitchen and dip into a plate of Mom's ravioli with Pop's special mystery-recipe sauce. Keep some hot for me! They say we'll be in Berlin soon.

Love,
Leo

Tony's letter wasn't as long. But since Tony almost never wrote home, Gabriella treasured it even more.

The guys were listening to shortwave radio and called me over to hear somebody named Gabriella Vivanti. Did I know who she was? When I said sure that's my sister, they bet me I was lying. So if we ever make it back from this crummy island, I'm going to bring five ugly-looking guys to meet Gabriella.

We're not fighting right now. Iwo Jima was tough, but we won. We're just sitting around waiting for . . . .

The rest of Tony's letter was blacked out by the censor, except for Tony's name at the bottom. But Gabriella thought she could guess what it contained. He would be landing on Japan next.

The newspapers said Japan would never surrender. To win the war in the Pacific, the United States was going to have to invade Japan. That would mean a lot more soldiers would get killed.

Because if the Japanese fought so hard to keep a tiny island like Iwo Jima, what would they do to defend their homeland?

The fighting was going hard in Europe too. The Allies were now in Germany, and the Nazis knew this was their last stand. Almost every day, Gabriella's friends at school talked about somebody else whose brother or father had been killed. In the windows of homes and stores, gold stars replaced the blue ones, one by one.

And then, on a Thursday afternoon, Pop came into the kitchen of the restaurant as they were getting ready for the evening serving. Gabriella was snacking on some mozzarella and dried-tomato salad that Mom was making.

Mom stopped slicing mozzarella as soon as she saw Pop's face. Gabriella looked up, and her first thought was that somebody had died. And then fear gripped her as she wondered: Which one? Tony or Leo?

The other workers in the kitchen stopped too. Pop was trying to catch his breath. Finally he looked around and said, "Roosevelt's dead. They just had it on the radio."

Nobody knew what to say. If somebody they knew had been killed . . . they were ready for that. But Roosevelt? The president? He couldn't be dead. Just last November, he'd been elected to his fourth term in office. He couldn't die before the

Roosevelt's funeral

war was over. He had been president for as long as Gabriella had been alive.

"How did he die?" Mom asked.

"They didn't say. He was down in Warm Springs, someplace where you go for your health."

"Rocco," Mom said, "we'd better close the restaurant."

He nodded. "Out of respect," he agreed. "Nobody's going to want to eat out tonight anyway."

But they did. People in the neighborhood and most of their regular customers showed up. When they saw the sign

Closed for the President's Death

on the door, they just knocked until Pop opened it.

"They're like our family," he said. "And a family comes together in times like this."

He didn't charge anybody for dinner that night.

Only three weeks later, the restaurant was filled again. This time people were laughing and singing. Bottles of champagne were brought up from the cellar. Usually, Pop served it only on New Year's Eve and for somebody's anniversary. The mood had completely changed. That day, May 7, the news came that Germany had surrendered. The war in Europe was over.

Gabriella was scheduled to broadcast that night. Originally she planned to have as her guest the head of the War Bond Drive. But he called to say he had to fly to Washington. So instead, she just talked all night to people from the audience. Everybody had a message for somebody they knew who was serving overseas: "Eddie, we're glad you're safe." "Ben, come home as soon as you can and I'll fix the best meal you ever had." "Carl, I waited for you and I'm still waiting."

Chicago celebrates the end of the war

Mom dragged Pop over to the microphone. All the time Charley had been doing the show, Pop had refused to go on the air.

"It's your restaurant," Charley had argued. "People would like to hear you."

"Then they can come here and talk to me like regular people."

It made Gabriella doubt the story that Charley's cousin Freddy always told: that Freddy and Pop stayed up for three days listening to radio signals when the *Titanic* sank. Because Pop didn't like the radio.

But tonight, Mom made him sit down with Gabriella at the broadcast table. "You have two sons out there somewhere," Mom said, "and they can hear you. So say hello to them."

He leaned over as if he thought the microphone were a snake. "Hello," he said softly. He cleared his throat. Gabriella didn't tell him you can't do that on the air.

"So we beat the Nazis," he went on. "That's good. We're all happy. You can probably hear the noise they're making here in the restaurant. Leo, you and your friends, you did a good job."

He trailed off. Mom poked him.

"OK, OK," Pop said irritably. "I got another son. He's out in the Pacific somewhere. We don't hear from him too much. Maybe that's part my fault cause we didn't get along always so well."

He cleared his throat again. Gabriella saw the sound engineer twisting dials to cut the noise. "Anyway," Pop went on, "for you and all the rest of you boys out there fighting Japan . . . your job ain't over. We didn't forget about you. Take care of yourselves, hear me? Tony? I want to see you back here too, so don't do anything dumb, hear me?"

He shook his head and got up suddenly. Gabriella thought he was about to cry. But she told herself she must be mistaken. He never cried.

ELEVEN

Discovering the Secret

PAPA'S REACTION TO THE NEWS THAT DAVID WAS missing was to lose himself in his work. He hardly ever came home before midnight, and sometimes slept on a cot in his lab. Mama, on the other hand, tried to pay more attention to Esther. Possibly Mama felt bad about burning Esther's notebook. Maybe it was just that she showered more affection on Esther to make up for losing David.

Esther had decided that David wasn't dead. The telegram had only said "missing in action." But an even stronger reason, to her, was that the thought of David didn't *feel* dead. It was hard to explain, but even when she and David were far apart, Esther knew she could listen hard and hear him talking to her.

She did that now, and she would hear things he'd written to her in the coded letter.

Esther had started to write in it again. She knew that it was wrong, but it was somehow important to her. For the past two and a half years she had lived in this strange place that was only a post office box. She wanted to know why.

Germany's surrender in May hadn't stopped the secret work at Los Alamos. There had been a few brief celebrations, but the next day everybody went back to work trying to build "it." Esther thought of what Dr. Oppenheimer had said about wanting to know how the world works. She decided that even if the war ended entirely, most of the scientists would go on trying to build "it."

Because they wanted to see if it could be done. Because they wanted to know what the secret was. Just as much as she did.

Mama spent part of the time trying to find out what mission David had been on when he was lost. The military commander of the Los Alamos project was General Leslie R. Groves. He was supposed to be very important. Sometimes Esther had seen him going by in a jeep. He was one of the few people who had his own driver.

But General Groves wasn't much help to Mama. He couldn't find out why David had left his safe job decoding Japanese messages.

General Leslie R. Groves

Esther knew why. David wanted to do something more than sit in an office all day. He was like Hans and his friends playing bomber pilots on the front lawn. He wanted to fight. So when he got the chance to parachute into China, he took it.

Esther thought about him floating down from the sky on the end of a parachute. It did look like fun when she saw it done in a movie, like sailing on the end of a white flower. And down below David were miles of flat green rice paddies. She'd seen a picture of them in *National Geographic*. That was the way she imagined China to be, with high mountains in the distance.

Maybe it was like Shangri-la, the hidden valley from the novel *Lost Horizon*. Where nobody ever grew old. If David had parachuted into Shangri-la, he would never be found. Esther wondered what it would be like if he wandered out of the valley many years later. She would be an old lady, and he would still be twenty years old, just the way she remembered him.

Summer came, and school was over. Esther had more time to investigate, although she couldn't carry the notebook outside. Something was up, she was certain. At night she could hear large trucks going in and out of the main gate to the laboratory area. The lights in the buildings there stayed on long after midnight.

The scientists seemed more excited too. At the PX people eating lunch talked in whispers. Once, when Papa and Mama were having a conversation, they stopped as soon as Esther entered the room. It wasn't fair, she thought.

Then Mama told her that she and Papa would be going away for a few days. "We can't bring you along, but Mrs. Dichter will take care of you."

"What do you mean, take care of me?" Esther hadn't forgotten that Hans's mother was the one who told Mama about the notebook.

"Well, they live right upstairs. She'll fix your meals. You'll have someone to play with, and if anything happens—"

"Hans and I don't play together, Mama. He's a boy." And a snitch, she added to herself. "As for meals, I can cook better than Mrs. Dichter. It's bad enough having to smell cabbage cooking without having to eat it."

"Well," Mother said, "it's just for a few days. But promise me that if anything happens you'll go right upstairs to the Dichters."

If anything happened. Esther nodded. "What about Mr. Dichter?" she asked.

"Oh, he's coming on this trip too."

So that was how Esther realized they were going to test "it." All over Los Alamos, people left in their cars, suitcases packed for a few days. The only adults who remained were military or civilians like Mrs. Dichter who weren't part of the scientific staff.

Esther was almost as unhappy as she had been when the telegram about David came. Now it was going to happen, and she wouldn't be there.

She decided to fix herself the meal she liked best: a thick hamburger. She went to the grocery store and asked the butcher to grind her half a pound of beef.

"It's just for you?" he asked as he weighed it.

"Yes," she said.

"Both your parents go off to the desert?" he asked.

She looked at him, and he put his hand over his mouth. But she could see from his eyes that he was smiling. "Whoops," he said. "I didn't say that."

So even the butcher knew.

At home, Esther pan-fried the hamburger until it was brown on the outside. She put the meat on a thick bun and poured ketchup on it. Then she added some dill pickle chips and sliced onion.

The desert, she thought. The butcher knew they were going to the desert. But New Mexico had a lot of desert. What part would they go to?

After finishing the hamburger, she went to the living room to find an atlas. It was heavy, and she put it on the floor to look at it. Lying on her stomach, she noticed something underneath Papa's favorite chair. She pulled it out. It was a road map.

It looked as if Papa had unfolded it and then not found the right way to fold it up again. He often did that. Esther spread it out and saw that it was a map of New Mexico.

Papa had marked it with red pencil. He had drawn a line on the road headed south from Santa Fe. Los Alamos wasn't even on the map—just a little road from Santa Fe that led nowhere.

Esther followed the line with her finger, far down almost to the Mexican border. It stopped at a town named Alamogordo. It was all by itself in the middle of a desert. The name of the desert was printed on the map: *Jornada del Muerto.* That was Spanish, Esther knew, for "Journey of Death." It must be a pretty dry desert to have a name like that.

The discovery excited her. Right away she got her notebook and wrote down the names on the map. Really she would have liked to have pasted the whole map in her notebook, but Papa might notice it was missing.

If only she could find a way—any way—to go there. The only transportation out of Los Alamos was by car or truck. She would have to get to Santa Fe if she wanted to take a bus. She wasn't even sure if there was a bus to Alamogordo.

And there was no one to ask. She heard voices upstairs and the footsteps of someone moving around. Suddenly the apartment seemed too lonely. She never minded being left alone before, but now she turned on the radio, just so there would be some noise.

She listened to dance music com-ing from New York. She tried to dance around the apartment, remembering the times she had practiced dancing with David. It probably wasn't any fun for him, but he did it anyway because she liked it. Maybe right now he was thinking of her. Maybe—

There was a knock at the door. Esther jumped as if it had been a pistol shot. Without even thinking about it, she ran to answer it. There wasn't anybody dangerous in Los Alamos, and in fact most people didn't lock their doors at all.

Esther had the strange feeling that David would be standing there. Miraculously unhurt, in his freshly pressed uniform, looking just the way he had when he'd left.

Instead, it was a woman Esther had never seen before. Esther was so surprised that she just stood there without saying a word. The woman was slim and dark, with her hair cut short. She had on a pair of dark slacks with a man's jacket, which some women had started to wear since the war began. And she was smoking a cigarette.

"Is this where Jack Aldrich lives?" she asked.

Something about the woman's voice seemed familiar, though Esther was sure she'd never seen her before. "Yes," Esther said, "but he's not at home right now."

The woman nodded and looked at her. She had piercing dark eyes that Esther felt were searching out secrets. Esther suddenly remembered that her notebook and the map were spread out on the floor.

"You must be Esther," the woman said, confirming Esther's fear that she was here to investigate.

"Why would you say that?" Esther said, imitating a movie she had seen in which Bette Davis played a woman accused of murder.

"Because I'm your father's cousin Peggy," the woman replied. "I've seen pictures of you at Aldrich House in Maine."

Esther blinked. "Well," she said. There was an awkward pause. "I guess you'd better come inside."

"Will Jack be back tonight?" Peggy asked. Esther had brought her a glass of iced tea. At the same time, she had picked up the notebook and map and put them out of sight.

"No . . . he and mother are gone for a few days. I'm sorry you came so far. There isn't any place for visitors to stay in. . . ." She tried to remember if it was still forbidden to tell anybody the name Los Alamos. "In fact," she said, giving Peggy a puzzled look, "I don't think we ever had any visitors here."

Peggy smiled. "I have press credentials, but it took a lot of arguing to make them let me come here. This place doesn't officially exist, you know. It isn't even on a map."

Esther nodded. "How did you find out about it?"

"Oh, I'm a real snoop," said Peggy. "You have to be if you want to be any good as a journalist. Something that's as big a secret as this . . . it leaves holes."

"Holes?"

"Yes. You know it's important because people don't want to talk about certain things. They get upset when you ask questions about it. That always points me in the right direction."

"Were you always like that?" asked Esther. "A snoop, I mean."

"Sure. When I was your age I used to spy on my own family. Because nobody would tell me anything."

Esther laughed, but it was a nervous sound. Peggy noticed.

"I guess that's what you do, huh?" Peggy said.

"I was trying to find out the secret of Los Alamos," Esther said quietly.

"And did you find out it was the atom bomb?"

Esther nodded.

"So is that where your parents have gone?"

Answering Peggy's questions was like pulling a scab off your knee. Esther knew she shouldn't, but she couldn't stop.

"I think so."

"Is that what's in the notebook and map you put away so I wouldn't see them?"

Esther smiled. There wasn't any use trying to hide things from Peggy. The best thing to do was try to get something for herself.

"If I show them to you," said Esther, "will you take me along?"

As Peggy pointed out, there was no time to spare. She gave Esther ten minutes to put some spare clothes in a bag. "I once had to get out of Paris when the Germans were marching into the other side of the city," Peggy told her. "*That* was a hurry."

Peggy had rented a Ford in Santa Fe to get to Los Alamos. On the way back, she took the sharp curves down the mesa faster than the military drivers did. But when she got on the straightaway on the other side of Santa Fe, she took off like a comet.

It was the most thrilling ride Esther ever took. "Where did you learn to drive like this?" she asked.

"Actually, your Uncle Harry taught me," said Peggy. "Did you know he was a race-car driver before he was a movie star?"

"Yes," said Esther. "I met him when we lived at Nell's house. But I think I remember her teasing Uncle Harry about a girl beating him in a car race. Was that you?"

Peggy chuckled, and downshifted to pass a truck going up a hill. "Yes, but it wasn't really fair. He was only driving a car. I was riding a horse."

Esther had to pay close attention to the driving because Peggy gave her the job of following the route on the map. Using a flashlight, Esther called out whenever they had to make a turn. From U.S. 85 to State Route 380 at San Antonio. Then onto Route 54 at Carizozo. Each time they started down a new road, it seemed to be narrower and less well paved than the one before. On some stretches they were on dirt roads that threw up clouds of dust. Small rocks hammered against the underside of the car. When the trip began, they had seen red taillights in front of them every so often, but for the last hour they could see only their own headlights disappearing into the darkness.

Finally they reached Alamogordo, a small town that looked as if everyone were asleep. Which was no surprise, since it was nearly 4:30 in the morning. "We need gasoline," said Peggy.

Luckily they found a station that was open all night. A man who looked Mexican came out to fill their tank and wipe the windshield.

"How far to the turnoff for Route 70?" Peggy asked him after a glance at the map.

"Oh, Route 70, you can't go out there," he said. "That's all military land out there."

"Is that right?" said Peggy. "I thought it was the *Jornada del Muerto*. We heard the sunrise is pretty over the desert."

He laughed. "Maybe it used to be. The military uses it to drop bombs and test weapons. You'd really be *muerta* if you went out there."

"Any way to drive around it?" she asked.

The man leaned through the window and pointed to a spot on the map. "Down around here is an old dirt road that bootleggers used in the 1920s when they smuggled whiskey in from Mexico. Kids sometimes go out there. But I don't know if you can get through to the other side. If anybody stops you, you didn't hear about it from me."

"Mum's the word," said Peggy, drawing a line across her mouth.

For the first time since Santa Fe, Peggy drove at a reasonable speed. They kept going past the big sign at the turnoff to Route 70. It read:

U.S. GOVERNMENT
PROVING GROUND
ADMISSION PROHIBITED

A few miles farther down the road, Peggy said, "There it is!" and swerved the Ford to the right. Esther grabbed the door handle to keep from falling. She hadn't seen anything that looked like a road, and as the car bounced up and down wildly, she was sure Peggy was going to get stuck.

But road or no, Peggy kept the Ford going forward, almost as fast as before. After about ten minutes, she slowed to a stop and then turned out the lights.

"Where are we?" Esther asked.

"We should be right on the edge of the *Jornada del Muerto*. And if any military police come by, we're just looking for a place to camp out."

"But how do you know if we're near the test?" Esther said.

"From what I know about it," Peggy replied, "we don't have to be near it to see it."

"Oh. So it was a big bomb after all. I didn't know if it would be big or small."

"The biggest."

They sat there for an hour. Peggy turned on the car radio, but the only station that came in was in Mexico. The music was lively and full of brass, but even so, Esther gradually drifted off to sleep.

She started to dream about David. He was sitting in Shangri-la having dinner with some Chinese people. Only everybody was speaking Spanish. When David saw Esther he waved and told her to sit down. "Have some food," he said, and even though he was speaking Spanish she could understand him. But a waiter brought a plate that had nothing on it but two large insects. "Watch out," said David. "They're poisonous."

She woke up then, wondering why anybody would serve poisonous insects. She rubbed her eyes and thought she saw the sun come up. "Oh, look," she said, turning to Peggy, "It's a beautiful sunrise after all."

Right after that, she realized it wasn't the sun. Or if it *were*, she was still dreaming. Because the shining disk of light on the horizon kept expanding faster and faster. It turned so bright that Esther put her hands over her eyes. Even then, the light was so bright that it shone through her fingers. She thought for a second that she could see her bones, like an X-ray picture.

She opened her hands a little to glance at Peggy. She was aiming a camera out the windshield, rapidly snapping pictures. "This is it," she murmured. "I'll get a Pulitzer Prize. Unless it doesn't stop."

Atom bomb explosion

Doesn't stop? Esther remembered something Papa had said about that. It was when Dr. Oppenheimer was there. "Limitless?" Was that what they were talking about? Did they mean this light could keep on getting bigger and bigger until. . . .

But then the light changed color. Esther peered at it again. It was yellow now, and there were reds and greens swirling inside it. But it was so huge! She didn't know how far away it was, but she could tell that it was as big . . .

Big as a city. They could destroy a whole city.

Suddenly Esther remembered that this was a bomb. A bomb that would be dropped on some place where people lived. And that there was nothing it couldn't destroy. Nothing at all.

I know the secret now, she thought. *I know why everything at Los Alamos is a secret. Why the people working there are so nervous about talking about "it." About the thing. They are all afraid of it.*

TWELVE

Secrets Kept

OCTOBER 1945

THERE WERE EVEN MORE ALDRICHES THAN BEN
had thought. It was fitting, of course, for all family
members to gather on such an important occasion:
to honor someone in their family who had sacri-
ficed his life for his country.

Ben was going to be part of the ceremony. He
would throw a floral wreath into the water at Burton's Cove where Uncle Georgie had last been seen.

The Aldriches were grateful to Ben. He had
been the only witness to Georgie's act of heroism.
But there was another reason, a secret one.

After Ben swam to shore and raised the alarm
about the German submarine, the police and fire

departments arrived. There wasn't any fire by then—just the charred, floating remnants of the Aldriches' boat, the *Board of Avon*. Uncle Georgie was never found, and there was no sign of a German submarine either.

Not surprisingly, the fire chief and the police chief—who were Pomeroys too, relatives of the town's mayor—refused to believe Ben's story. In fact, when they learned he was a Japanese American, they were suspicious of him.

Uncle William and Uncle Nick cleared Ben. They were certain that only one person could have dreamed up the plan of chasing German submarines in the middle of the night with a 20-foot motor launch. And they identified the battery-powered submarine detector net as an idea that could only have been Georgie's.

The Aldriches weren't certain, however, that Georgie had actually seen a submarine. "Well," said Aunt Maud, "he clearly ran into something. Our boat was destroyed."

"Perhaps a reef," suggested Uncle William.

"No," Ben insisted. "I saw it. It moved. It was gray and shone in the darkness."

The matter might have ended there except that the Aldriches heard that the Pomeroys were making fun of Georgie. According to one of Aunt Maud's friends in town, Mayor Pomeroy said Uncle Georgie was dangerous and should have been locked up years ago.

That was something the Aldriches couldn't tolerate. It was true, they themselves had made fun of Georgie's inventions over the years. But when someone outside the family did that, the Aldriches closed ranks.

The trouble was, they couldn't think of a way to get back at the Pomeroys. "We could announce the cancellation of the annual free theater production," suggested Aunt Anna.

"Father wouldn't approve of that," said Uncle William. Even though Lionel Aldrich, the father of William and Maud and Georgie, had been dead for forty-three years, they still made decisions based on what he might have done.

"You know, this is really the sort of situation where Georgie would come up with an idea," said Uncle Nick.

That was when Ben remembered what had happened on the drive down to Burton's Cove. "I know what he was going to do," he said, "just as soon as he finished off the German submarine."

He told them what he and Georgie had seen at the Pomeroys' house, and how Georgie knew the Pomeroys were hoarding gasoline.

Uncle William and Uncle Nick looked at each other. "You thinking what I am, Nick?" asked Uncle William.

"Let's get out the Packard and pay the Pomeroys a little visit."

Ben never learned exactly what William and Nick said to the Pomeroys. But the next day Mayor Pomeroy proclaimed that the town would have a ceremony honoring Uncle Georgie for saving Maine from the Nazis.

Before that could take place, however, Japan surrendered. That was August 14, a week after the United States had dropped atom bombs on the cities of Hiroshima and Nagasaki. Japan had no defense against them.

Nobody was quite sure what an atom bomb was. President Truman called it "an instrument of mass destruction." Reading the newspapers, Ben realized that it had taken only a single bomb to destroy each city. He shook his head, trying to understand that.

Everybody said it was a good thing that the United States was the only country to have an atom bomb. Nobody cared very much about the thousands of people who had been killed. After all, they were Japanese. And the Japanese had attacked first, hadn't they?

Ben had a secret thought that he kept to himself. Mother had cousins who lived in Nagasaki. Of course, Mother hadn't heard anything from them since the war started. But it seemed likely that they must be dead.

Ben's secret thought was: Maybe it would be better if no country had a bomb that could destroy a whole city. But with all the people waving flags in town, with everybody cheering the end of the war, he knew better than to say that out loud.

In the days before the ceremony, the rest of the Aldriches started to arrive. Ben had trouble keeping them all straight. First to arrive was Jack, his wife Sara, and their daughter Esther. When the family heard Jack and Sara's other child, David, was missing in action they wanted to include him in the memorial service.

But David's sister protested. "He's not dead," said Esther. "It wouldn't be right to hold a memorial for him."

"There's no sense arguing with Esther," her father said with a weary smile. "She was able to overcome all the security surrounding the most secret project of the war. If she thinks David is alive, maybe he is."

"We read Peggy's articles about the atom bomb," said Aunt Maud. "I thought it was nice that she mentioned your name, Jack."

"It was my fault," said Esther. "I told Peggy. . . ."

Jack shook his head. "I was planning to resign, anyway," he responded. "The work was done. I want to go back to teaching now."

Ben could hardly believe it. This mild-looking, slightly bald man with glasses—he'd been one of the people who built the atom bomb. Ben wanted to ask why, but he knew that was a silly question.

Peggy arrived next. She was a journalist, Ben knew. She had described what the first atom bomb test looked like. Even though she waited to publish her articles until after the bombs were dropped on Japan, everybody wondered how she had gotten the story. Peggy and Esther gave each other a wink, and Ben figured it out.

A day later, the two most famous Aldriches, Nell and Harry, arrived. Harry had recently learned to fly a plane from his friend Clark Gable. He expertly landed a seaplane on Lake Chohobee, just at the foot of the hill by Aldrich House. Inside,

in addition to Nell, were the Vivanti family, long-time friends of the Aldriches.

Last to get out of the plane were two young men in uniform. Leo's army jacket displayed corporal's stripes, and Tony wore a handsome Marine uniform. Rocco, their father, stood around accepting everybody's congratulations as if he had been the one to fight the war.

Tony said very little, but when he was introduced to Jack Aldrich, he shook his hand warmly. "You probably saved my life," Tony said. "If we hadn't dropped the A-bombs, my unit would have been in the first wave invading Japan."

Jack just nodded. "I'm glad you made it back," he said.

Tony's brother Leo whispered in his ear, and Tony's face changed. "I'm sorry that your son didn't make it," he told Jack.

"We all did what we had to," Jack replied. His voice dropped so that they could barely hear him. "He felt he had to take risks."

The Vivantis had a daughter too. "I'm Gabriella," she said to Ben. "You don't look like an Aldrich."

Ben explained how Nell had saved his family from the detention camps.

"So you must be the kid who saw the Nazi sub," said Gabriella.

Ben nodded. He didn't want to be the center of attention.

"That's a great story," said Gabriella. "You want to come talk about it on my radio show?"

"You have a radio show?"

"Yeah, unless Charley wants it back. But he's still in Europe, as far as we know. We heard he was wounded. Whether I keep the show depends on Freddy. He's coming up from New York with his family tonight."

Freddy arrived in a prewar Buick limousine with his wife and their two young children. They brought a couple of surprise guests too.

"It's Molly and Polly," Aunt Maud shouted when she saw them. "My baby girls!"

Ben couldn't tell who she meant. For a second, he thought Aunt Maud was talking about Freddy's children.

But no, the baby girls were two middle-aged women. One wore a WAAC captain's uniform. The other looked as tan and weatherworn as if she'd spent twenty years in a jungle.

As Ben learned, she had done just that—hunting for new species of insects in South America. Dr. Polly, as she introduced herself, started to talk about her work. Nobody paid much attention until she opened a box with holes in it. Something that looked like a blue hummingbird as big as a bat flew out. Only it wasn't a bird or an animal. It was a huge insect.

Loud screams followed as there was a mad scramble to get out of the flying thing's way. That only frightened the creature. Beating its wings frantically, it started to flail against a windowpane.

All at once Tony stepped forward and held out his arm. "Don't hurt it," said Dr. Polly. "It's perfectly harmless."

"It's looking for a perch," Tony said. "I saw a whizzbang like this in the Solomon Islands." Sure enough the flying creature landed on his outstretched arm and rested there, pumping its wings slowly.

"You did?" Dr. Polly said. "I thought it was a new species that hadn't been discovered before. I was going to give it a name—*Diplax Aldrichensis.*"

A whizzbang

"Well, in the Solomons we just called 'em whizzbangs," said Tony

The children, who were a little more curious than the adults, took a few tentative steps forward. Tony held his arm in Gabriella's direction. She forced a smile and slowly reached out. The thing jumped from Tony's arm to hers. In a minute, Ben and Esther were letting it land on them too.

Nonetheless, Aunt Maud insisted that Dr. Polly put it back in its box and then lock it in Freddy's automobile. After dinner, Uncle William and Uncle Nick took a stroll down to the garage to see that everything was shut up tight.

When they returned, everyone was sitting on the sunporch having dessert and coffee. Ben's mother had fixed hot chocolate for the children. For the first time since 1942, there had been plenty of real chocolate for sale in the stores.

The screens on the sunporch had already been taken down for the winter and replaced by glass storm windows. Sitting here, the Aldriches and their guests watched the moon throw reflections on the water.

Conversations gradually slowed to a stop. Everybody seemed to be thinking of somebody who wasn't here. The war was over, but the Aldriches had lost some of their own along the way.

Nell's voice broke the silence. "I'm just counting heads," she said. "And I think we're all here except Charley."

"David," said Esther. "David is still on his way back."

Nobody replied. Esther knew they were thinking the same thing Mama had told her—that if David hadn't been heard from by now, he probably was never going to be found.

They heard a car turn into the driveway. Esther jumped up from her chair. "Maybe that's him now," she said.

But it turned out to be a surprise of a different kind. It was Charley, walking with a cane. His left foot was heavily bandaged. A dark-haired young woman held his arm, helping him up the steps.

Charley and his mother Peggy exchanged glances. Gabriella put her hand over her mouth, remembering the last time she'd seen them together. She hoped that another staring contest wouldn't break out.

But no. "Mother," Charley said, "and everybody else. . . ." He gestured around the room. "I am back from the war and this is my wife Jeanne."

Jeanne

There was a shocked silence. Aunt Maud broke it by asking loudly, "What? What did he say?"

And then everybody remembered their manners, hugging Jeanne and congratulating Charley and talking all at once. Gabriella sneaked a glance at Peggy, who looked dazed, but smiling.

The next day, Ben's mother was busy. She had to fix breakfast for twenty-five people. The house was nearly full. It took more than an hour for everybody to finish eating and get ready. Aunt Maud changed her dress three times because she couldn't decide whether it would be a sunny or a rainy day. Finally they got into the cars, being careful to leave the insect box in the garage, and drove down to Burton's Cove.

A crowd had already gathered—townspeople, friends of the Aldriches, and those who were always ready to turn out for an occasion when there might be a free bean supper afterward. The sky was gray, but the water a deep blue. White-caps lapped against the shore, and a cold wind was blowing in from the sea. Everybody buttoned up their coats as they stepped on board a fishing boat that had been donated to honor an Aldrich.

Several other boats accompanied them. One held Mayor Pomeroy and his family, who looked grumpy that they had to come out for the occasion. When they reached the rocky point where the lone pine tree grew, the pilots cut back on the motors.

The rocky coast of Maine

Mayor Pomeroy gave a short speech, which was hard to hear. It would be reprinted in the weekly newspaper anyway. Aunt Maud handed Ben a wreath she and Anna had made. Red, white, and blue ribbons were entwined with lilies and pine branches. Across the wreath was a white ribbon with a gold star on it, and the words:

GEORGE ALDRICH 1874–1945

As Ben stepped forward, someone said, "Look! There's a whale!" Everybody turned. It

A whale spouting

was a familiar sight to those who lived along the shore, but still an awesome one. Farther out beyond the mouth of the cove, the massive creature, its gray skin shining smoothly, rose above the water. Suddenly a spout of water spurted from it, high in the air.

It reminded Ben of something he'd seen before. His hands clenched the wreath a little tighter. If he'd seen the whale on a dark night, it might have looked like a submarine. And the water spout, if it had been dark, could have seemed like a periscope.

He pressed his lips together. That was something else Ben would never tell anyone. As he leaned over the rail to drop the wreath in the water, he thought to himself, Uncle Georgie was a very brave man anyway.

Esther watched the wreath sail downward. As it touched the water and began to float away, a shock went through her. David, she thought, don't go. Then, for the first time, she realized that she wouldn't see him again. Not ever. Tears came to her eyes, and she turned away from the railing.

Gabriella saw Esther cry, and put her arms around her. She wasn't sure why Esther was crying, but she knew when people needed to be comforted. Gabriella was feeling a little guilty today, because her brothers had both come back alive. She felt glad about that, but didn't tell anyone. It wasn't right to be glad, she thought, when so many people had lost those they loved. She watched the wreath float out to sea.

A Few Historical Notes

The United States entered World War II after Japan attacked the U.S. naval base at Pearl Harbor, Hawaii, on December 7, 1941. The next day, the United States declared war on Japan, and Japan's allies Germany and Italy then declared war on the United States.

World War II was the most devastating conflict the world has ever seen. By some estimates, 45 million people, civilian and military, lost their lives in the war. More than 400,000 members of the United States Armed Forces were killed.

One reason the United States and its allies won the war was the industrial might of the United States. Many women went to work in the factories making weapons, tanks, trucks, and other war materials. Everyone shared in the war effort by cutting back on their consumption of much-needed materials. As you read in the story, the government issued ration books that limited the amount of gasoline, certain kinds of foods, and other materials such as tires, that people could buy. Women stopped wearing stockings, because the silk was needed to make parachutes.

No Japanese Americans ever committed any acts of sabotage or disloyalty. However, on February 19, 1942, President Roosevelt issued Executive Order Number 9066. It gave the War Department authority to relocate all persons of Japanese ancestry. (A small number of Americans of Italian or German descent were also detained.) The areas from which Japanese

Americans were to be moved included all of California, Washington, and Oregon, as well as part of Arizona. Ten detention camps were set up in remote areas as places for the relocated Japanese Americans to live. Surrounded by barbed wire and guarded by soldiers, these were American-style concentration camps.

Despite the violations of their rights, many Japanese Americans volunteered for the U.S. armed forces. The majority served in the all-Japanese 442nd Regimental Combat Team, which was the most decorated unit of its size in U.S. military history.

During the 1930s, many European scientists moved to the United States because they feared the growing power of Nazi Germany. One was Albert Einstein, already known as one of the world's great scientific geniuses. In 1939, Einstein wrote President Roosevelt a letter warning that new developments in physics made it possible to build "extremely powerful bombs of a new type." Einstein knew that German scientists might already be working on such bombs. The letter led to the establishment of the Manhattan Project, the code name for the effort to build an atomic bomb. In 1942, General Leslie R. Groves was placed in charge of the project. He appointed a civilian, Dr. J. Robert Oppenheimer, to head the scientific effort. Laboratories were built on the site of a former boarding school at Los Alamos, New Mexico. After three years of work, the first atomic bomb was exploded near Alamogordo, New Mexico, on July 16, 1945.

As you may have guessed from the story, some scientists feared that the nuclear reaction that was the heart of the bomb might be uncontrolled, and in theory could have destroyed the world. Calculations showed there was only a small chance of this happening, but there was no way to know for sure.

On August 6, a U.S. bomber dropped an atomic bomb on Hiroshima, Japan. Three days later, another A-bomb hit the city of Nagasaki. More than a hundred thousand people were killed in the attacks, and more died later from radiation poisoning. Five days later Japan agreed to surrender.

Peggy Aldrich is a fictional character. The first news story about the atomic bomb was written by William L. Laurence of *The New York Times*. The U.S. government invited Laurence to watch the test at Alamogordo, and later even permitted him to ride on the plane that dropped the atomic bomb at Nagasaki.

The Vivanti Family

Rocco (1900–   ) m Teresita (1902–   )

Tony (1923–   )   Leo (1924–   )   Gabriella (1932–   )

The Tamura Family

Kenji (1911–   ) m Michiko (1913–   )

Ben (1931–   )   Iris (1932–   )

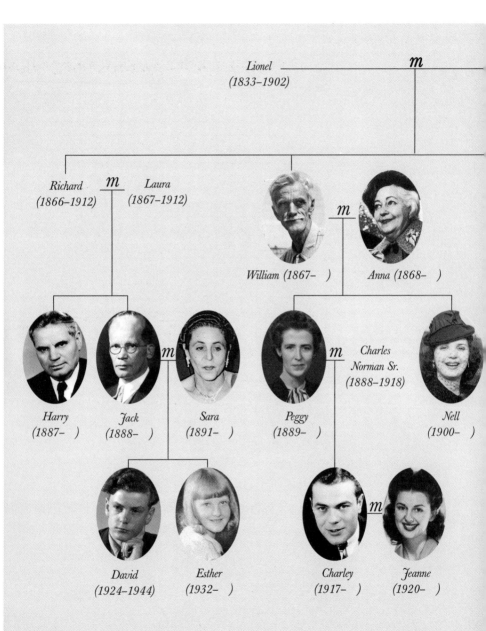

The Aldrich

Lionel
(1833–1902)

m

Richard
(1866–1912)

m

Laura
(1867–1912)

William (1867–)

m

Anna (1868–)

Harry
(1887–)

Jack
(1888–)

m

Sara
(1891–)

Peggy
(1889–)

m

Charles
Norman Sr.
(1888–1918)

Nell
(1900–)

David
(1924–1944)

Esther
(1932–)

Charley
(1917–)

m

Jeanne
(1920–)

Family

Adele
(1838–1910)

Zena
(1840–1919)

Maud (1872–   )

_m_

Nick Woods (1870–   )

George (1874–1945)

Molly
(1898–   )

Polly
(1898–   )

Freddy
(1899–   )

Things That Really Happened

1940

The first issue of *Batman* comics is published.

President Roosevelt becomes the first president to be elected to a third term of office.

1941

On January 1, the first FM radio stations go on the air.

On December 7, Japanese planes bomb American ships and naval base at Pearl Harbor, Hawaii. The following day, President Roosevelt asks Congress to declare war on Japan. Germany and Italy, Japan's allies, then declare war on the United States.

Charles Moulton, a comic-book artist, creates the superheroine Wonder Woman.

At the end of December, rationing of automobile tires begins. Because rubber will be needed for military vehicles, the sale of tires to civilians is restricted. In the war years, other materials, as well as food, will be rationed.

1942

On February 19, President Roosevelt signs Executive Order 9066. It orders the removal of all Japanese Americans in the western states to internment camps. Some Americans of German and Italian descent are also interned by the government.

Rationing of sugar and coffee begins.

Gasoline rationing in eastern states begins; each family is allowed three gallons a week for "non-essential driving."

During the Years 1940–1949

President Roosevelt approves the Manhattan Project, a secret effort to build an atomic bomb.

The first American jet aircraft is tested.

1943

Congress repeals the Chinese Exclusion Acts, laws from the 1880s onward that kept Chinese from immigrating to the United States. The repeal is prompted by the fact that China is the United States' ally in the war against Japan.

Rationing of canned goods, fresh meat, fat, and cheese begins.

April 8, President Roosevelt freezes all wages, prices, and salaries.

Long-distance telephone calls are limited to five minutes.

1944

On June 6, D-Day, the United States and its allies invade Nazi-controlled Europe. The largest invasion force in history lands on the beaches of Normandy in France.

1945

On April 12, President Roosevelt dies.

On May 8, Germany surrenders. World War II in Europe ends.

On July 16, the first atomic bomb is tested at Alamogordo, New Mexico.

On August 6, a United States plane drops an atomic bomb on Hiroshima, Japan. Three days later another is dropped on Nagasaki. These are the first and only uses of atomic weapons in warfare.

On September 2, Japan's representatives sign a surrender agreement. World War II comes to an end.

1946

Returning servicemen start families with their wives. The birthrate in 1946 is 20 percent higher than in 1945. This is the beginning of the "Baby Boom."

Congress passes the G.I. Bill of Rights, which provides financial help for war veterans in education, housing, and business. At least four million veterans receive benefits under the bill.

Former British prime minister Winston Churchill, in a speech at a college in Missouri, coins the phrase "Iron Curtain" to describe the dividing line between Soviet-controlled Europe and the democratic countries.

1947

On March 12, President Truman announces a "containment policy," in which the United States will help the governments of Greece and Turkey fight communism. This is one of the first steps in what later came to be known as the "Cold War" between the Communist and democratic nations.

Jackie Robinson of the Brooklyn Dodgers becomes the first black player in major-league baseball.

Peter C. Goldmark of CBS Records develops the long-playing $33\frac{1}{3}$ rpm phonograph record.

Edwin Land develops a photographic process that will later be sold as the Polaroid Land Camera, in which the picture develops inside the camera in about sixty seconds.

On October 5, President Harry Truman becomes the first president to speak to the American people via television.

1948

Margaret Chase Smith, a Republican from Maine, becomes the first woman to be elected to the U.S. Senate.

1949

On March 2, a U.S. Air Force plane, the *Lucky Lady II*, completes the first nonstop flight around the world.

Builder Abraham Levitt and his sons create the first Levittown on Long Island. This is a housing development in which every house is built from prefabricated materials, bringing costs down. Houses in Levittown sell for $7,990 apiece.